LISA SUZANNE

NO MISTAKE
VEGAS ACES: THE WIDE RECEIVER
BOOK FOUR
© 2022 Lisa Suzanne

All rights reserved. In accordance with the US Copyright Act of 1976, the scanning, uploading, and sharing of any part of this book without the permission of the publisher or author constitute unlawful piracy and theft of the author's intellectual property. No part of this book may be reproduced or transmitted in any form or by any means, electronic or mechanical, including photocopying, recording, or by any information storage and retrieval system without the written permission of the author, except where permitted by law and except for excerpts used in reviews. If you would like to use any words from this book other than for review purposes, prior written permission must be obtained from the publisher.

Published in the United States of America by Books by LS, LLC.

ISBN: 9798352792520

This book is a work of fiction. Any similarities to real people, living or dead, is purely coincidental. All characters and events in this work are figments of the author's imagination.

BOOKS BY LISA SUZANNE

VEGAS ACES
Home Game (Book One)
Long Game (Book Two)
Fair Game (Book Three)
Waiting Game (Book Four)
End Game (Book Five)

VEGAS ACES: THE QUARTERBACK
Traded (Book One)
Tackled (Book Two)
Timeout (Book Three)
Turnover (Book Four)
Touchdown (Book Five)

VEGAS ACES: THE TIGHT END
Tight Spot (Book One)
Tight Hold (Book Two)
Tight Fit (Book Three)
Tight Laced (Book Four)
Tight End (Book Five)

A LITTLE LIKE DESTINY SERIES
A Little Like Destiny (Book One)
Only Ever You (Book Two)
Clean Break (Book Three)

Visit Lisa on Amazon for more titles

DEDICATION

For my three favorite people.

CHAPTER 1

Tristan

"Come on in," Mrs. Taylor says, and I follow her into the kitchen, where I slide into a chair at the table.

I refuse to believe this is history repeating itself despite the very convincing thoughts in my brain telling me that's exactly what this is.

"Why is she in Chicago?" I ask. I can't hide the alarm in my voice.

She shrugs, and she seems wholly unconcerned—a total contrast to the waves of fear that continually ripple down my spine. "I came home to this note yesterday that she was going to visit her friend Sara in Chicago for the weekend," she says. She slides the note over to me, and yep...that's all it says. "Probably something to keep her mind occupied while you were out of town. She got the clearance to travel, so she decided to travel."

"I get that, but she's not answering her phone. I've tried calling and texting a hundred times," I say. "It's just not like her."

"Oh, you know how girls are," she says, brushing off my concerns. "They probably got to talking and catching up and she left her phone in her purse or something. She didn't want to bother you for your big weekend, but I'm sure she'll call soon."

I wish I felt more relief than I do. I wish I could let my future mother-in-law brush away my concerns so easily.

She's not worried, but I just can't shake the gut feeling that something is off here.

"Do you have Sara's number by chance?" I ask.

She tilts her head. "No, I don't. I'm sorry."

"What about her address?" I just came from the airport there, but maybe I can turn around and go back to Chicago and find her or help her. I just want to be whatever she needs, and I feel so goddamn helpless sitting around waiting.

She shakes her head. "They lived in an apartment together, and I have that address, but Sara and her fiancé bought a house when the lease lapsed. I don't know where." She pauses, and then she pats my hand as she asks, "Can I get you anything?"

I shake my head. "No, thanks. I'm going to head home. Let me know if you hear from her, okay?"

She nods. "Of course," she says.

Maybe I'm overreacting. Maybe this is just some new territorial thing since I feel so fiercely protective of her. I head out the front door, and it's as I'm stepping onto the front stoop from the house that something white catches my eye near the shrubs. I pick it up.

It's just a part of a ripped sheet of paper, but I can piece together enough partial words to figure out what this is.

—rmination of Paren—

Dr. Camer—

It looks like the termination of rights my lawyer sent over to Cameron Foster. But why would it be *here*? And why would it be just one part of one page like the entire document was torn into shreds right here on this very porch?

The mystery deepens, and while a sense of relief washes over me to have one answer, rage fills in the gaps.

Was he here?

No **MISTAKE**

Is that why she ran off to Chicago?

It still doesn't tell me why she isn't answering my calls, and I have more questions than answers now…but I have a clue, and that's better than where I was a few minutes ago.

I run next door and head in through the side door of the garage. I'm two seconds from looking up this Cameron Foster asshole and delivering a message to him myself in person…but then I realize it's Sunday. He's not going to be at the practice where she worked. He probably won't even be at the hospital, and I'm sure someone of his stature goes to great lengths to protect his personal information and privacy, much like myself.

That's where our similarities end, though.

Fuck.

I could go to Chicago and try to figure something out, or I could just stay here and wait for her.

I want to fucking punch something right now—Cam's face would be a great start—but instead I draw in a deep breath through my nose and let it out through my mouth. I repeat the drill three times as I will a sense of calm to wash over me.

It's not effective, but it's a start.

I head inside, where I find my parents sitting at the kitchen table. They're not eating, and as I look over at their faces…they look like they're in the middle of a serious conversation.

"What's wrong?" I ask immediately.

They glance at each other again, and then my dad turns toward me. He blows out a breath and clears his throat. "I found out yesterday morning that the cancer is back."

His words plow into me like a fucking brick to my stomach.

It feels like someone's kicking me when I'm already down.

"Fuck," I murmur, sinking into one of the open chairs at the table. "How bad is it?"

He shrugs and averts his eyes to the table, and it's strange seeing my father this way. He's always been the strong one, the brave one, the courageous one…the man I've tried to model my own life after. But right now, he looks…scared. "It's just another spot in a new location. It hasn't metastasized, but they want to extract it quickly. They've got me on the schedule in about ten days. The doctor is talking about chemotherapy or immunotherapy after that depending on how much they get during the surgery."

"That's good news, then, right?" I ask. "That it's just another spot and hasn't spread?"

My mom nods. "That's what I told him, too," she says, reaching across the table to squeeze his hand.

"Then what's wrong?" I look back and forth between them.

"It's just disheartening, that's all," my dad says, and my heart sinks into my stomach.

He's scared. It's not easy for him to admit it, but he has to be.

And I am, too.

How many more times will this happen? We can hope and pray, but he just went through this three months ago, and now he has to go through it again. There's nothing to say it won't happen again and again, and the thought of him going under the knife every three months is terrifying.

Each time might make him a little weaker, and then what? What'll be left of the man?

"It's scary, Dad, but you've got Mom and me right here," I say. "Chemo or immunotherapy or whatever comes next, we've got this. You're a fucking fighter, and I'm not letting you quit on me."

My mom tears up at my words, and my dad looks a little choked up, too…which makes *me* feel a little sting behind my eyes.

I break the silent sadness by cracking a joke. "Let's go chop some wood or something."

He chuckles. "Let's do it."

We head out to the garage, and he grabs a few projects that need sanding while I head over toward my weights.

"You and Mom should move to Vegas," I say quietly as we're each working on our own thing together.

"Thought about it," he says, "but with this melanoma thing, I don't know if the desert with all that hot sunshine is the best place for me."

"Fair point," I say. I once looked up how many sunny days there are in Vegas versus how many in Iowa, and there's over a hundred more days *per year* of sunshine in Sin City. "You better get your ass on the plane to come watch me play, though."

He chuckles. "You know I'll be at every game I can possibly be at. And if I can't be there, your mother will."

"You'll both be there," I say, forcing an even tone despite the emotion clogging my throat.

They've never missed a home game in all my years playing football, from peewee league through today. I'm sure as hell not letting him start now.

CHAPTER 2

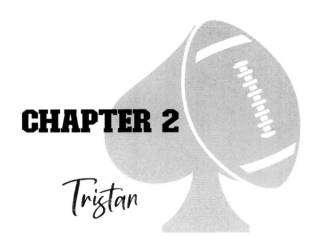

Tristan

I don't know what to do with myself, and so I run.

I run on the treadmill until my legs burn, and it's still not enough.

I can't seem to put a stem on the worry filtering through my veins. I'm worried about Tessa. Worried about the baby.

Worried about my dad.

My hamstring seems totally healed, and the weather's nice enough today that I decide the treadmill isn't cutting it. I tighten my shoes and head the opposite direction of Main Street, cutting through backyards and cornfields because I don't want to run past the house on the corner. I don't want to think about everything it means.

I'm running away from it.

I'm trying to push away the fear. Janet doesn't seem worried, so I shouldn't be, either.

Still, I found that little scrap of paper and I don't know what happened next. Maybe I should show Janet, or maybe I just need to wait it out another day. Maybe I should call Cameron Foster and ask him why a scrap of paper with his name on it was sitting in front of Tessa's house, or maybe he wouldn't know anyway.

I just don't know what to do. I turn to run toward the river, and I keep running almost at a sprint until I find myself walking along the dock and flopping down onto our bench at the scenic overlook.

I should've brought some water with me as I gasp for breath after my sprint through the backside of town.

I don't like that I'm here without Tessa. It feels somehow wrong, like this is *our* place and being here without her is somehow doing a disservice to her memory.

I hate that I'm worried.

I hate that I can't get a hold of her. I hate that she's not picking up her phone. I hate that I think she might be ignoring me.

I really hate my traitorous thoughts that she left me again, that she's not coming back, that this is all some response to me leaving her here alone while I went off to Vegas to party.

I wish I would've gotten a punching bag for my parents' garage because I feel like I could work out some major angst on that shit right about now.

She'll be back. In my heart, I want to believe this. I want to believe that it's just some misunderstanding. Maybe she forgot her phone charger, though I suppose there'd be easier solutions for that than complete radio silence.

But my head keeps telling me she ran away again.

The thought makes me want to fucking tear something in two.

We *just* got back together. We just confessed our true feelings. We just started letting each other in again.

We just…we just…we just.

None of it matters.

The only tiny shred of hope keeping me from falling completely off the cliff right now is the fact that Janet isn't worried. She knows where Tessa is. She told me where Tessa is. She's not suffering from fits of anxiety the way I am, and I was hoping my run would calm down those thoughts, but it hasn't.

At all.

Especially not when I'm here on our bench. I run a fingertip over the rough edges of the *T+T* carved into the wooden slat. "Fuck," I mutter as a little sliver of wood embeds itself in my finger.

So running my finger over rickety old wood was a bad idea. Noted.

As the pain of a sliver darts through my hand, a strange thought pulses in my mind.

I can't help but think about how I want to use some of what I learned at Coax to punish Tessa for putting me through this once she's back. Cutting off all contact after she left me all those years ago is a big deal, and I need her to know that. She can't just disappear on me.

I can't take it.

I remember Troy Bodine's punishment for Sapphire when he withheld her pleasure.

Tessa's on pelvic rest…but I'm not.

There are plenty of creative ways to let her know she shouldn't do this ever again.

I'm making plans for when she returns. Because this time, she *will* return, and it won't take seven years for me to find her again.

I inspect my finger a little more closely as I start to catch my breath, and my gasping turns to softer panting. I see the tiny sliver sticking out and use the nails of my thumb and forefinger to grasp it out, tossing the offending shard to the ground.

And then I hear a voice behind me.

"I don't know if I've ever seen you sitting on that bench all by your lonesome." I whirl around and see Tiffany Gable standing there.

Great. Just fucking great.

"Everything okay?" she asks.

I stand as I draw in a breath, and then I move toward the wooden railing in front of me and rest my palms on it, locking my elbows straight as I lean on it.

I do this because I know Tiffany, and I know she'll sit on that bench next to me.

Nobody gets to sit beside me on that fucking bench except Tessa.

Nobody.

"Everything's fine," I lie through a clenched jaw.

"Where's your girl?" I hear the wooden floorboards creak with her footsteps, so I know she's moving closer to me.

"It's none of your business," I mutter, keeping my eyes on the water rather than on her.

"Did she run away again? Did things get too serious for her? Because if she did, you know, I'm…*available*. Like last time, if you know what I mean." She moves in beside me but doesn't touch me. I can picture her winking in an exaggerated way at me, and I move my hands from the railing.

"I know what you mean, and I'm going to have to respectfully decline." I start to walk away.

"I heard you proposed," she says to my retreating figure. "You sure that's a good idea?"

I stop and turn to face her. "I'm sure it's none of your business."

She shrugs. "Didn't you just get divorced like five seconds ago? Don't you want a chance to…explore your options?" She leans forward a little, and I can see right down her shirt—exactly as she planned, I'm sure.

No MISTAKE

My eyes don't flick there. I may be a tit guy, but I only want Tessa's tits. Definitely not Tiffany's. I *never* wanted Tiffany's, even when I supposedly got to have them.

"Why do you know so much about my life?" I ask instead of answering her questions.

She cackles. "Everybody knows everything about everyone around here."

I shake my head. "That's not true. I don't know what *you* have been up to, for example."

She hoists herself up so she's sitting on the railing, and she leans forward to give me that shot down her shirt again.

I continue to hold strong against looking.

"Ask away," she says.

I shake my head. "See, that's the thing. I don't care."

I turn to walk away again, and her voice stops me. Again.

"You should care."

I grunt out a laugh. "Why's that?"

"You'll see." She winks at me, and I just shake my head as I start my run back toward home.

I've got enough things to worry about right now.

Tiffany Gable and her ominously veiled threats are not on that list.

CHAPTER 3

Tessa

"Ugh!" I yell in frustration as I stare at the blank screen. I finally decided to ask Sara to take me over to Best Buy on Sunday morning so I can take a look at new phones. I've had the damn thing sitting in rice for the last thirty-six hours, and I don't even know why I let Christine scare me into taking this God-awful road trip, but I did.

In my head, my intent was to protect my baby at all costs.

Now I just wish I'd never come.

I didn't realize how freaking dependent I was on my phone until I dropped mine in a toilet at a rest stop.

That's right. I'm that freaking stupid.

I stuck it in my back pocket when I got out of the car since these maternity jeans don't have front pockets, forgot about it, went to the bathroom, and sure enough, just when I stood up, it slipped out right into the urine-filled water.

I almost threw up as I fished it out, but I managed to hold it together as I ran to the sink to rinse it off. Half a bottle of sanitizer later…and the damn thing wouldn't turn on.

When I got to Sara's, she stuck it in rice to dry it out, and now, a day and a half later, I wish I never would've left Fallon Ridge.

I tried to send my mom an email, but I couldn't remember my password. Why do I need to know it when it's stored on my phone and in my laptop?

I didn't bring my laptop. Didn't think I'd need it for a quick trip to convince Cam, who I haven't even seen yet, to sign over the rights to the baby. My plan was to call him when I got into town and ask him to meet me somewhere.

But I don't know his number.

I don't know *anybody's* phone number. Who memorizes numbers anymore when you just type them into your contacts and save them?

I had Sara send my mom an email through the address listed on the church website, but chances are pretty likely my mom won't see it until Monday morning since she rarely checks her email, particularly on the weekend outside of regular business hours. And I don't think Tristan and I have even exchanged email addresses, so I can't have Sara email him to let him know my phone's dead.

So we play the waiting game.

"Did you back everything up to the cloud?" the salesperson asks me.

I have no freaking clue. Is he for real? "I don't know."

"Once you log into your account we can check."

"Log into my account?" I echo. "I don't know my password."

"You don't know your password?" he repeats.

I shake my head.

He sighs.

This is going to be a long day, and it's only Sunday morning.

I think about going home and just coming back during the week to confront Cam, but what's even the point? I came here to see him, and I'm going into the office with Sara in the morning to tell him to sign the damn papers.

No MISTAKE

At least that's my plan.

I'm terrified, though. Christine made it seem like he wants to be part of this baby's life. Or she wants him to be, anyway.

I'm not sure why she got involved.

She knows nothing about this...that much was clear.

Why she didn't just call me, I'll never know. Maybe she wanted to see my pregnant belly for herself. It's a mystery to me.

But I'm fighting for this baby. I'm fighting for the dream life that was within my grasp a few days ago. I'm fighting for Tristan, me, and Fallon to become a family.

I'm fighting to keep Cam out of it forever.

I had to do it alone. Tristan's not home, and my first thought was just to get the hell out of town. I called Sara as I left my house, and she told me to come stay with her. She told me she'd help me put together a plan. I beelined for her place.

It's not like Tristan's back home anyway. It's the final day of his big party, the day when everyone checks out and heads home. I'm sure he'll be worried when he gets home and I'm not there, but my mom will show him the note I left. Everything will be fine.

Sunday feels interminable. I'm nervous to see Cam, and even though Sara is doing her best to entertain me, I can't stop thinking about tomorrow.

What if he sees my rather enormous baby bump and decides he wants to be part of her life?

What will I do then? What will Tristan and I do?

Christine is right, though. Cam does have rights even though he told me in no uncertain terms that it was my problem.

I left my job to protect the baby. I went back to Fallon Ridge to get away from Cam. I did everything right, and all I needed was his signature on the papers Christine somehow intercepted to make everything legal.

Instead I'm spending my weekend incredibly stressed and I don't even have Tristan's calming voice in my ear telling me everything's going to be okay because I dropped my damn phone in the toilet.

What a mess.

"Let's go shopping," Sara suggests after I've paid for the phone I can't activate since I don't know my account details. "Some retail therapy always makes me feel better."

The salesman gave me instructions to take it home and activate it there. He told me he could do it in store, but it might take a few days to recover my account. I'll be home tomorrow, so I opted out of that one.

I agree to the retail therapy, and a few hours later I have a trunk filled with baby clothes and toys. I found the sweetest little purple bedding set with unicorns and flowers—very fairy-esque and somehow magically princess-ish at the same time, and as soon as I saw the set, I knew it was perfect for my baby girl. She picks up a few outfits for her honeymoon, which is just a few months away now, and we shop until dinnertime, when we go out for some Chicago style pizza.

If I wasn't already huge from carrying a baby, the pizza would do it. I eat so much I feel like I'm carrying twins.

Once we're back at Sara's new house, which is gorgeous, by the way, I take a short, relaxing bath and head to bed.

I toss and turn all night, which is no different than usual at seven months pregnant, and when light dawns in the morning, I take a shower and get ready to see Cam.

Nerves crawl down my spine, and I can't seem to keep still. I pace back and forth as I wait for the clock to hit seven-fifteen when Sara and I agreed to meet in the kitchen for breakfast.

No MISTAKE

This is not keeping things low stress, but this is something I have to do.

I know I need to eat something, but my stomach is in knots. I draw in a deep breath and release it slowly, trying to calm my racing heart down.

There are so many what-ifs in my head right now, but I know worrying about them is useless. I'll have my answers soon, and then we can take it from there.

"Want eggs or something?" Sara asks once I join her. "I've just been having protein shakes these days."

"No, don't go to all that trouble. Do you have yogurt?"

She nods and hands me a little individual container of vanilla Greek yogurt, and then she grabs me a spoon.

We sit at the table together.

"Tell me more about Tristan Higgins," she says, clearly trying to distract me as I eat and she drinks. "I know the basics—you met when you were twelve, he was your next-door neighbor, you broke up shortly before you graduated high school, and you reconnected when you both found yourselves in your hometown at the same time a few months ago, and now you're engaged to be married and he has agreed to raise the baby with you as the father. But what's he *like*?"

I shrug. "I don't know. He's Tristan. He's a normal guy who happens to play football professionally, but to me he's still the boy next door who I fell in love with when I was twelve."

"That's the sweetest thing I've ever heard. Is he, like, *so good* in bed? He seems like he would be. He gives off this vibe like he knows what he's doing. It's in the way he walks or something, like he's packing heat down there and has to adjust his gait to accommodate the size."

I giggle. "Pretty much all that, yes."

She laughs.

"And he's so kind. He's the type of guy who would do anything for anybody. He leaves things better than he found them. He always wants to help, like he's got some savior complex or something."

A thought occurs to me as I say the words.

Is that why he wants to be with me?

Is he trying to *save* me and the baby the way he helps everybody else?

I'm not sure why I'm questioning it right now of all times. I know he loves me…but *why* does he love me? Why does he want to give up the single life he just got back? Why does he want to raise somebody else's baby as his own?

Is it because it's what he truly wants? Or is it because he sees a girl he used to care about in a tough situation, and he's doing what he thinks he has to do to help me?

The thought leaves me feeling a little empty and a little broken.

"Okay, girl, what's the plan? Are you just going to walk into the office all pregnant like *hey everyone, surprise! It's Cam's baby in here!* Or do you have another plan?" she asks.

I chuckle. "Gosh, I've missed you."

She reaches over to squeeze my hand. "I've missed you, too."

"I don't know if I have a plan. I didn't really think about seeing Paul while I'm there or explaining what's going on," I admit.

"Let's get there early, then. You can just be waiting in Cam's office when you get there. It'll be a nice little surprise for him."

I chuckle nervously, and then I nod. "It's a plan."

CHAPTER 4

Tessa

My heart pounds as I pack up my overnight bag and toss it into my car. I follow Sara toward the office, and as I navigate there, the pounding picks up the pace until it's a thunderous roar as I pull into the old, familiar parking lot.

I need to get this right. I need to walk out of this place with a signed set of papers…only I don't have the papers, and I doubt Cam does, either, considering his wife stood on my front porch and rage ripped them to shreds.

I think back to her words on the porch. I didn't pass out, exactly, but everything went black for a second and I thought I was going to. I held onto the doorframe until I gulped in enough air to remain standing, and she didn't bother asking if I was okay.

Instead, she said, "Half that baby is his, and as much as I hate that fact, hate him, hate *you*, it's the truth. You can't just make him sign away those rights."

"Have you spoken to him?" I asked her. "He told me to take care of it. He doesn't want anything to do with this baby. He wanted to keep it a secret so he could win his precious award, and I quit Lakeshore so I didn't have to see him every single day and work with someone who was such an asshole to me."

She gave me a look like she didn't believe me. "He would never. He loves children, and he'd never hurt one…especially not one of his own."

"You don't know him as well as you think you do," I told her.

"Listen, little girl. Neither do you." She spun on her heel and headed back toward her car. She opened her driver's side door and tossed out her final words. "We'll be suing for full custody. Better to allow that child to grow up in a loving family than to a single mother in this joke of a town." Then she got in her car and drove away.

My first thought was that the courts often side with the mother. But Christine might be right. Certainly a judge would look at our situations and choose the successful, established doctor with a wife and four kids to raise the baby over a single, unemployed mother.

But I won't be unemployed for long since Ellie is taking me on at Prince Charming Public Relations. And I won't be single for long, either, since Tristan has proposed to me.

Even now as I drive toward Lakeshore Pediatrics, the thought that he only proposed to me because he wants to save me pops back into my mind.

Well, if he wants to save me, maybe he needs to save me a little faster. If Cam and his wife truly plan to sue me for full custody, they'll have a harder time if I'm married—especially to someone who is far wealthier than Cameron Foster.

I pull into the familiar parking lot I've pulled into hundreds of times, but this time is so very different. I look around the lot. Cam's car is here. Paul's is not.

Perfect.

Sara and I head inside together, and she squeezes my arm in solidarity before I head down the hallway toward Cam's

No MISTAKE

office. I take a deep breath just outside the door, and then I move into the doorway.

His eyes flick up to mine before they move down to my swollen stomach.

"Nurse Taylor," he mutters, and I can't tell if it's animosity, hope, or fear in his hushed tone.

"We need to talk."

He sighs and pushes aside some papers on his desk, taking his glasses off and rubbing the bridge of his nose before he nods once. "Come in. Close the door."

I do as I'm told.

In the old days, *close the door* was a sure signal I was about to get banged.

I'm not sure what it means today, and I'm terrified to find out.

I slide into the seat across from his desk.

"How've you been?" he asks.

"As if you suddenly care," I mutter. "Can you please explain why your wife showed up on my doorstep threatening to sue me for full custody?"

He presses his lips together. "She found the papers your lawyer sent. Went a little ballistic."

"Have you, uh...have you had babies with other women?" I ask.

He shrugs. "I've been accused of fathering other children, yes. Whether it was true remains to be seen, and whether those women had their children or not is none of my concern. I was planning to sign and send the papers, but she took them and punched the address listed as yours on the paperwork into her GPS and took off. She thought you were being an asshole by asking me to give up my rights. She never asked me what I wanted." He rubs the bridge of his nose again, and for a moment, I think how stressed he looks.

Things must be a little strained at home.

Or maybe he's used enough women in this city that he isn't getting his needs met the way he's used to.

"And what *do* you want, Dr. Foster?"

His eyes lift to mine, and he looks confused for a moment, like nobody's ever actually asked him that and he's never really considered it before. I get the vivid sense he's tied to his wife the same way Tristan was tied to his, but while Tristan actively sought a way out, Cam doesn't bother. Instead, he cheats on her and gets his kicks where he wants but still goes home to her.

It doesn't make sense. If that's what you want to do, just break up.

But there's kids involved. That must be why he stays. If she's so adamant about him getting custody of *my* baby, I can only imagine how she'd be about her *own* children if it came down to it.

"What I want doesn't matter. I have a reputation to uphold, responsibilities to tend to, and a job to perform. Have your lawyer send over the papers via email. I will send them back via Docusign so Christine cannot intercept them again." He gives me a semi-tender look that I'm not used to seeing from him.

For the briefest flash of a second, I think I understand him a little better than I did before.

But then he opens his big dumb mouth again. "I don't want to take your child away from you. I don't want anything to do with you *or* the child, so I'm glad to sign over my rights."

"What about Christine?" I ask dryly, more out of morbid curiosity than anything else.

"Let me worry about her," he says firmly. "Is there anything else?"

No MISTAKE

I draw in a deep breath. "Yes. My phone is dead and I need hard proof you're not going to fuck me over. Look up Richard Redmond in Nevada and get in touch now asking him to email you the papers."

He gives me a surprised look, and then in a shocking twist, he actually does what I ask. He taps a few buttons on his computer, and he makes a phone call. He puts it on speaker so I can hear, too. It goes to voicemail. "You've reached the office of attorney Richard Redmond. Please leave a detailed message with contact information."

"This is Cameron Foster. I was served some legal papers from your office not so long ago regarding paternity of Tessa Taylor's unborn child. Please send the papers again via email as well as to my office address." He rattles off his contact details along with a callback number, and then he hangs up.

He glances at me. "Good enough for you?"

I shrug and stand. "It'll do. Have a nice life." I turn to walk out of his office, but his quiet voice halts me.

"Is it true that you're marrying that Higgins kid?" he asks.

I turn back to face him, and I snag my bottom lip between my teeth. Baby girl chooses that moment to kick me in the ribs, and I wince as I rest a hand over my belly. "That's none of your business."

He clears his throat, and he pushes to a stand behind his desk. "I know it's not my place, particularly after I cut ties and didn't offer you anything to help with raising the child, but I just want to make sure you're both taken care of. I may be an asshole, and I may not deserve to know the answer, but I'd like to know."

"You can stop calling her *the child*," I snap. "It's a girl, and fuck off with your fake concern. We'll be fine." I spin on my heel and storm out of his office with my head held high.

Paul still isn't in, and maybe it's for the best. I want to get back home anyway.

I hug Sara goodbye, and then I head out to my car, the weight of the world suddenly lifted from my shoulders.

CHAPTER 5

Tessa

The nearly three-hour drive from Chicago back home feels endless. I don't have my phone plugged in playing my favorite tunes, so I'm stuck with the radio—which is largely commercials the entire way back. I spend more time flipping through stations trying to find a song than I do actually listening to music.

Tristan's truck is in the street when I pull onto Oak Tree Lane, and I pull into my mom's driveway off to the side so she can slip her car past mine and into the garage when she gets home from work. Before I've even cut the engine, Tristan is storming across his driveway, and as he approaches my SUV, he looks some combination of anxious and angry.

He opens my door for me, and he practically hauls me out of the seat and into his arms.

"Fuck, Tessa. I was so worried." He cradles me in his arms, and I'm no lightweight with the extra baby weight, but he holds me as if I weigh nothing.

"I'm sorry," I say, tears filling my eyes as I spot the worry in his melt into something else.

Something...hotter.

"Inside," he grits out. "Now."

"I dropped my phone in the toilet and it killed it and I had to get a new one but I didn't know my password or anybody's number so I couldn't call and—"

He cuts me off by pressing his lips to mine. "You can explain later." He carries me to the door, and I don't know if I've ever seen him like this. He sets me down so I can unlock the door and open it, and then he takes my hand and practically drags me down the hall to my bedroom.

"You think I was off in Vegas cheating on you with those other women?" he demands once he slams the door shut behind me.

"I, uh…I—" I find myself at a loss for words, but I realize my last text to him said something along those lines.

"What will it take for you to see that *you* are the only woman I want to be with?" he asks.

"Why?" I whimper.

He looks caught off guard. "Why what?"

"Why do you want to be with me?"

His brows knit together. "Because I love you. Because we are connected down to our very souls. Because there's no other woman who understands me the way you do, who loves me the way you do, who makes me feel the way you do. Because you were my best friend when we were kids, and you've slipped into that spot again, and I can't imagine another day without you as my wife."

I'm floored at his description. In a lot of ways, it's the same way I feel about him…and I'm not sure why I didn't trust that when I was away from him.

It's easier to believe the doubt, I guess.

"I got it in my head that you only wanted to be with me because you feel this need to save me," I say softly.

His jaw drops open just slightly for a beat, and he looks like he wants to say something, but then he closes his mouth. He works his jaw for a beat, clenching it with some unnamed emotion. "When I got back here and you were gone, all those feelings from seven years ago washed over me. It was like the first time you left all over again. I didn't know where you were. I couldn't get in touch with you." He shakes his head, and he looks a little unfocused…a little *lost* as he says the words. "I was terrified."

"I'm so sorry, Tristan. I'll never leave you again. I promise."

"I think you deserve to be punished," he says, and he grips his belt buckle. "Don't you?"

Punished?

Is he, like, going to hit me with his belt? He wouldn't do that.

He unbuckles it and pulls it off.

Would he?

He tosses the belt on the bed.

"Answer me," he demands.

"Um, ye—yes," I stammer. "But I don't know what you mean."

He unbuttons his jeans and pulls down his zipper, and then he pulls out his cock. It's hard and throbbing and red, and he strokes it a few times. My eyes fall onto it, and I can't help but stare as he strokes himself.

"God dammit, why are you still on pelvic rest?" Despite the way he's acting, all dominant and forceful, his eyes fall tenderly on me. This is a new way for him to show me love, whatever this is, and an ache presses roughly between my thighs.

"Get on your knees," he demands, and I do it.

Eagerly.

This is a brand-new Tristan. A brand-new Tristan I can get behind.

Or one I want to get behind *me*.

"That's my good girl," he praises, and I swear to God I preen under his compliment.

He pulls my shirt over my head, and then he flicks the hook of my bra in the back and pulls it off me. As he works, his cock is at eye-level. It's thick and hard and pointed straight up, and my mouth waters. I have this sudden urge to please him, like pleasing him will please *me*, too.

He pauses to take a step back, and he looks down at me. I feel self-conscious for a beat as he gazes at my swollen stomach that seems to get bigger by the day, at my breasts that don't seem as perky as they were a few months ago.

"Perfection," he murmurs as he studies me. I sit up a little taller on my knees at the approval. He presses a fingertip softly to my chin. "Open."

I gasp a little at the command, but I drop my jaw anyway. He fists his cock again, and then he slides it into my open mouth. "Mm," he hums. "That's right. Wrap those pretty pink lips around me."

I open my mouth wider to accommodate his size, and he slides it in until it hits the back of my throat. My eyes start to tear up at the feel, and he pulls himself out. "Take it all, baby," he murmurs, and he closes his eyes as he leans his head back, his neck corded, as he pushes back in.

"Now suck," he says.

I do as I'm told, and he moans a little louder, so I suck harder.

"You look so beautiful on your knees sucking my cock," he says, and his words cause that ache between my legs to intensify.

It's nearly unbearable. I wonder for a beat if this is considered *rest* when I'm this freaking wet.

I need some relief, but I can't get it because of doctor's orders.

But being here, sucking on Tristan's cock as he groans with pleasure, as he tells me how beautiful I am and compliments how I'm doing this…it's filling some void I didn't know existed within me.

"You have no idea what you're doing to me," he murmurs, and he thrusts into my mouth a little harder as he holds the back of my head.

I'm helpless on the floor, his cock practically choking me, and all I want to do is be very still so he can take me in whatever way he wants. Whatever way he *needs*.

I've never been like this with anybody. This is new. Different. A little terrifying, if I'm being honest, but also possibly the hottest thing I've ever experienced in my life. I'm pleasing him with my mouth, and he's pleasing me with…his words?

I didn't know that was a thing. I didn't know I could be so turned on just by the things he's saying to me.

We've established a trust between us. I know he'd never do anything to hurt me, and I keep that in mind as he grips onto the back of my head with both his hands and drives his cock in and out of my mouth.

He pants as the pleasure washes over him, and at the last second, he pulls out of my mouth and strokes his cock, a loud growl erupting from his chest as hot white streams of come spill onto my chest. My eyes are wide as I watch it shoot out of his cock with each pulse that shudders through him, and I don't know if I've experienced a hotter moment in all my life.

All I want in this moment is to reach down and rub away the ache pulsing between my legs.

"Fuck, that's hot," he says, eyeing the messy paint project he just made of my body.

Tristan hauls me up into his arms and sets me down on my bed. He pulls his shorts on then walks out of my room. He returns a moment later with a wet washcloth and a cup filled with water, which he sets on my nightstand. He sets to gently cleaning the evidence of his orgasm off my chest.

"That didn't really seem like a punishment," I whisper while he works.

He chuckles. "How badly do you want to come right now?"

I clear my throat. "Pretty bad." My voice is hoarse and strangled.

"*That* is the punishment, Tessa."

"Oh," I gasp. I think I get it now. I think about asking whether he's done that before, but then I realize…I don't really want to know.

I don't want to think about him with other women, telling them the things he told me just now.

I want it to be something special that just happened between us.

I want to be his only *good girl*.

CHAPTER 6

Tristan

God *damn*, that was hot.

Her on her knees, her perfect tits bouncing with her movement, her mouth open and taking me all the way to the back of her throat as her eyes widened, the squirm as her body reacted to my words...these are images that will live rent-free in my brain for the rest of time.

"Are you okay?" I murmur, a little afraid I hurt her. I wipe the final remnants of my come off her chest, and I grab her shirt and bra from the floor, setting them on the bed beside her.

Now comes my favorite part of the post-sex bliss: taking care of my girl.

She nods. "That was...whoa. It was hot, Tristan."

I chuckle as I set the washcloth on the nightstand and hand her the cup of water. I sit beside her on the edge of the bed, gently running my fingertips along her thigh. She sits up a little to take a drink. "You did so good. You were so gorgeous on your knees taking me all the way in."

I think for a beat I should tell her about the third floor of Coax. Maybe she'd understand, and it's in the past anyway. I had the opportunity to go this past weekend, and I didn't take it.

Maybe when she's in Vegas with me, we can go together. Maybe we can be the couple in the viewing room doing what we just did for an audience, or maybe we can be voyeurs together and I can run my hand up her thigh as we sit on one of the black leather loveseats together watching.

As I press a kiss to her forehead, though, I realize it's all wrong. We're older now, sure, but that doesn't mean she's ready for all that. She's sweet. I'd call her innocent, but the life growing inside her is proof she's not. She's not ready for the things she might see on the third floor, although the easy way she took direction along with the squirm that proved my words of praise turned her on tell me she might come around to it.

Her cheeks are flushed. "Thanks," she murmurs.

"Did you like it?" I ask.

She nods. "It was…different. You're usually so sweet, so tender, and even though this was more forceful, I knew I could trust you and you'd never do anything to hurt me. Somehow that understanding between us felt more intimate than normal sex."

I chuckle. "Normal sex?"

"You know what I mean." Her cheeks are still red, so I encourage her to take another sip of water.

She moves to put her bra and shirt back on, and I hand her each article as she needs it. I climb into the bed beside her.

"What was your favorite part?" I ask.

She shifts a little. "I feel weird talking about it," she says.

"Why?"

She shrugs. "Probably because I grew up in a home where we didn't talk about those types of things. Sex, intimacy…it was taboo. You didn't talk about it." She sighs. "And now we all know why. My father kept all sorts of topics off limits because he was scared we'd find out the truth about him."

"With me, nothing's off limits. Ever. You understand?"

No MISTAKE

She nods.

"If you liked something, or if you didn't, or if you want me to try something, or if you don't…it's all on the table." I reach over to take her hand in mine, and then I think better of it and tug on her so she's lying on her side, her face near my neck on the pillow and her arm tossed across my torso.

"I liked when you had both hands on the back of my head and you were shoving yourself into me." She says it in a mumble, her eyes down on my hand where I'm stroking her arm rather than on me—like there's something dirty or wrong about admitting that.

"I liked that, too," I say gently. "I liked how good you took it. I liked how I could feel the back of your throat with my cock, and I loved when you hummed a little while I was in your mouth. I don't even think you knew you were doing it, but you were lost to the moment, and it was so damn hot." I grab my dick over my shorts and readjust myself a bit. "I'm getting hard again just thinking about it."

Her eyes lift to mine. "Really?"

"This is what you do to me." I pull her hand over to feel for herself. "Only you, Tessa Taylor. It's always been you, and I want you to get it out of your head right now that there was ever anybody else who even compared. I want you to get it out of your head that you're just some project of mine to save. You're not. And if you don't believe me, I'll punish you again and again."

She squirms again. "Like you just did?"

I don't miss the hope in her tone.

I shrug. "I can be very creative. And I'll be honest with you, my love. This right here? This post-orgasm bliss where I can take care of you and make sure you enjoyed it, where we talk and you tell me whether I met your needs—mental and emotional to the best of my ability, and when it's safe, physical as well—this is the piece of sex that's most intimate to me. It's the most important part to me. It's the part where our souls connect instead of just our bodies."

She sighs, and it's a soft, sweet breeze of a sound, like she's breathing in my words and holding them in her heart. "Were you like this with—" She stops herself short.

"With…" I ask, trailing off at the end of my sentence.

"With your ex-wife?"

I shake my head. "No." I didn't learn about aftercare until I joined Coax, and I was done having sex with my ex-wife by that point. Nothing about my connection with Savannah was ever this intimate, and certainly not in the post-orgasmic moments.

She nods. "Okay. Good."

"Would it upset you if I had?"

She shrugs. "You said it's the part where souls connect, and the thought of your soul connecting to hers like that leaves me feeling a certain way."

"I've never connected with anyone the way I've connected with you," I say. Even other women I've taken care of…my soul never latched onto theirs the way it does with Tessa. I don't know how else to explain it, but it's like we were two people destined for each other.

"Is there anything else you want to talk about?" I ask.

She opens her mouth to say something, and then she seems to think better of it and closes it. She shakes her head.

I think about asking if she's sure, but whatever's playing in her head will eventually come out of her mouth. I have a feeling she wants to know more about where I picked up my newfound skills, but I'm not ready to tell her about Coax yet…or ever.

"What about you?" she asks. "As hot as that was, I feel like there's something on your mind." Her eyes search mine, and it's sort of incredible how connected we actually are—how well she knows me to know that I'm holding something back.

God, I love her.

"My dad's cancer is back," I say.

"Oh, Tristan," she says softly, stroking my cheek gently. "How bad is it?"

I lift a shoulder. "It hasn't metastasized, so that's good. He said they're operating next week to remove it." I sigh. "It's just…he just went under the knife, you know?" I swallow loudly to try to keep the emotions coursing through me at bay. "He just got rid of it, and the three-month check is when he's supposed to be all clear."

"I know," she says softly, soothingly. "And we can pray that the next three-month check is all clear."

I nod. "I'm not ready to lose him, Tess." I just got Tessa back after losing her. I'm not ready to lose someone else so important to me, especially not when the loss of him would be permanent.

"You won't." Her tone is fierce as she presses her lips to my jawline. "Not yet. But you can be by his side and spend as much time as you can with him. You can help him through it. You can be strong for him, and when you come home to me, I will hold you in my arms while you break down."

I lean down to kiss her lips. "Thank you," I say softly. I blow out a breath, feeling a little spent after that conversation. I turn the tables on her. "Tell me about Chicago now."

"I didn't go to visit my friend," she admits.

"I didn't think you did."

"Christine Foster, Cameron's wife, found the papers your lawyer sent over. She came here to confront me." Her tone is flat, and I can't help but wonder how she feels about the whole thing.

"What did she say?" I ask, my brows pushed together in concern as I try to keep my own feelings out of this.

That's my baby.

I know we don't share blood, but I've already come to love her as if we do. I could never even imagine telling a woman to just get rid of a child the way he did to her.

Just the thought of it still causes rage to pulse through me, and the thought of him having any part of the baby's life makes my stomach twist and bile rise in my throat.

He can't. Not after the things he said to Tessa. He doesn't deserve a single second.

"She told me they were going to sue for full custody." She glances up and meets my eyes. "And then she tore up the paperwork from your lawyer on my front porch."

I snap my fingers. "I found a scrap of paper by the shrubs when I was checking in with your mom to see if she'd heard from you."

She nods, and she lifts a palm to my cheek. "I'm so sorry I worried you."

"Let's put it behind us," I suggest. "I wish you wouldn't have gone alone to Chicago. If you would've told me—"

She holds up a hand. "What? You would've gone for me? You would've talked to Cam yourself?" She shakes her head. "Thanks, Tristan, but I can handle my own problems. I know you just want to help, but if you're constantly trying to jump in and save the day, you're not letting me live my own life. And there has to be that give and take in any relationship, don't you think?"

I lean over and press a kiss to her cheek. "You're right."

"I handled it anyway." She tucks some hair behind her ear. "I confronted Cam this morning and he left a message with your lawyer to send another copy of the papers. He said he will sign them before his wife intercepts them this time, and he said he doesn't want to get in my way. *Our* way."

"I'm proud of you," I say softly. "I know you can handle it. I know you don't need me, but it's still nice to feel needed. I still want to do what I can to help you."

She reaches over and grabs my face in her palms. She presses a kiss to my lips. "You do. Every single day. You make me feel loved and appreciated and worshipped, and I hope I do the same for you."

I kiss her, and I never want this moment to end. "You do. Only ever you."

I feel the weight of those words. I lost my way with Savannah for a minute, but the truth is that it *has* only ever been her. I've looked. I've sampled. I even joined a damn sex club trying to find the sort of connection I had with Tessa, and I never found it until I found her again.

She lets out a soft sigh and then we kiss a long, slow, tender kiss that only strengthens the words we've said here today.

CHAPTER 7

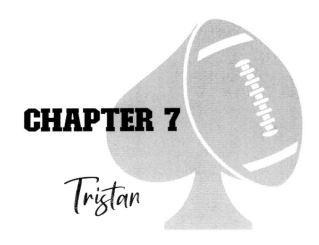

Tristan

I stare at the text for what feels like hours even though it's only been a couple minutes since it came through.

It feels like the second one fire goes out, another one pops up somewhere else.

It's getting exhausting, quite frankly.

I just unpacked my suitcase and stepped out of the shower at my parents' house when I heard the text come through.

Unknown: *Have you told your fiancée about your time at Coax yet?*

It's from a Vegas area code, but I'm not sure that matters.

Maybe I should just tell Tessa about it. I'm not sure it's even that big of a deal. So I'm a member of an exclusive, members-only club where sex happens. Okay, fine…a *sex club*. But I never fucked anybody there, and her accusation that I only want to be with her because I want to save her sort of meshes with the things I learned about myself in my time on the third floor at Coax.

But then I remember my vow to myself. It was always going to be my dirty little secret. I never wanted anybody to find out, and the more I think about it, the more certain I am that Tessa should never know…especially not after I ran into Brandi when I was in Las Vegas.

I just don't think she'd understand. She's on the conservative side. She was raised the daughter of the town pastor, and I feel like she'd never see me the same again.

Maybe it's true…maybe I do have a savior complex, and maybe I get off on stepping in to save the day. But that doesn't mean that's why I want to be with Tessa.

I want to be with Tessa because of the things I said to her.

I had plenty of opportunity to be with other women over the last few years—the last few months in particular. I wasn't holding out for Tessa, which should be obvious given the fact that I married another woman, but I *was* holding out to find the sort of connection I shared with her. I wanted to feel the way she made me feel. I wanted to experience that deep bond with somebody the way I did with her.

We haven't set a wedding date yet.

With the doctor's wife finding out about the baby and threatening to sue for custody…paired with my dad's illness showing me how short life is…on top of the constant threats coming my way courtesy of my ex…*plus* all the different people trying to break the two of us up—I'm starting to think we should do it sooner rather than later.

I can't lose her again.

I realize marriage doesn't mean I won't, particularly given the hell my last marriage was, but if we're legally tied to one another, she'll have a better shot at custody if the doctor comes after her. We'll have a better shot of making it through the Savannah threats or the Stephanie break-ups or the Tiffany manipulations or whoever it is that sent me this text this morning.

I delete it.

It's not worth responding to, but somebody somewhere knows I went to Coax. Somebody somewhere knows what happened.

No MISTAKE

And I'm quite sure it's not something Tessa needs to know.

It's almost like whoever sent it can sense I deleted it because another one comes through.

Unknown: *I'd be happy to inform her about your savior complex even on the third floor.*

My first thought is somehow Savannah found out.

But I know her number, and besides, she wouldn't hide her intentions. This isn't her style.

Don't engage, I tell myself.

Unknown: *I'm sure she'd love to hear all about what went down with Brandi in particular.*

I wonder for a second if this *is* Brandi. I got to know her, and I trusted her, and she's a member, too, so she signed the same legal paperwork I did about contacting members outside of the club.

But she wouldn't do that.

At least…I don't *think* she would.

Maybe I brushed her off faster than I should have back at the bash Ben threw for me in Vegas.

And it was another reminder that these people exist outside of Coax. In some ways, the world seems so vast, but in others…it's a small world.

I was raised with that small town mentality where everyone knows everything about everyone else until the one girl I cared about disappeared. Then nobody seemed to have any answers—or they trusted that whatever the town pastor was telling us was the truth.

If only they all knew.

Besides, I did seemingly disappear from the club as if from out of nowhere. I'd been going nearly weekly until the season ended, and then I came up here, reconnected with Tessa, and the rest is history.

I don't know what to say. I don't want to engage, so I block the number.

And that's when I remember something I found out in Vegas.

I download the JustFans app and find the profile Cory showed me.

Tessa Taylor, age 25, Chicago, Illinois. Engaged to NFL wide receiver.

The profile picture is definitely Tessa, and now that I'm home and can think for a second, I realize I've seen the photo before. I open Instagram and navigate to her account, where I spot the matching photo almost immediately.

I glance at the clock. It's five minutes until window time, and I think I should just be honest with her. I don't want to upset her, especially not when life in general *has* been stressful lately and she's supposed to be avoiding stress.

Still, she should know. This is something we should face together.

I report the account as impersonation, but I don't imagine that will stop whoever this is.

She's getting into position in her window, so I open mine.

"Can we talk about something?" I start.

Her brows knit together, and she nods. "Anything."

"Cory showed me something while we were in Vegas, and I think you should know about it."

Her hand moves to her chest. "Me?"

I nod.

"What is it?"

I toss my phone on the bed from where I sit. Best to just get this out there, right? "Someone's impersonating you online," I blurt. "They're using one of your images for their profile on JustFans."

"*JustFans?*" she screeches. "The porn site?"

"I mean, it's not *exclusively* porn, but yeah, that subscription site where creators can charge for original content," I say.

"What am I doing on there?" she asks a little dryly.

"I don't know. I haven't paid to see, but there are little underwear dances meant to be teasers to get users to purchase more. I'm sorry, Tess." My voice is quiet.

"What does *more* mean?" She looks like she's about to vomit.

I shrug. "She'll maybe pull on a bra strap so you think she'll ditch it in the paid portion. Maybe tease with her panties to make you think she'll touch herself."

"And she's pretending to be me?" she asks. "But…why? How?"

"She's only showing her body. Her hair could pass for yours, like she styles it the same way as you. As for the why…I don't know. And I don't know the *who*, either. I've reported the account, and I plan to have my lawyer look into it more. We can file a police report if you want."

"Stephanie," she hisses. "She cut her hair like mine. She dyed it, too."

"Why would she start up a JustFans impersonating you?" I ask.

Her fingertips move to her forehead, which she rubs for a second as she thinks. "I don't know. Between her daddy issues and her totally obsessive personality, I can't quite figure out why she does anything she does."

"You really think it's her?"

She shakes her head with disgust. "I'd need to see it, but she's the first person who came to mind who'd want to mess with me."

I nod. I don't say anything more, but I can see the fear on her face.

Now that our relationship is public, Stephanie—or even Tiffany and Savannah, for that matter—are hardly the only people on Earth who'd want to mess with her. With *us*.

I suppose one option is to just quit now. It would be the easy way out even though it would be much, much harder than last time.

But nothing worth anything comes easy.

It might be an option on paper, but it's not an option for us. We've fought to hell and back to get to where we are now, and I refuse to give up. I love Tessa. I love *our* baby. I love our future.

I will slay every single one of the monsters myself if I have to. As long as her hand is planted firmly in mine, we can get through anything.

As soon as I have that thought, I pray I'm not jinxing us.

I pray I'm not tempting the universe to bring its worst.

When you're going through something, you always think it's the worst thing—that you can't handle any more piled on top of what you're already dealing with. What doesn't kill you…and all that, I guess.

But I have a feeling all this is far from over, and I never imagined these would be the easy problems. I never imagined how much more would be piled on or how much harder things would get.

I never imagined there would come a time when we'd give up the fight for each other.

For *us*.

CHAPTER 8

Tessa

"Show me," I say.

His brows dip.

I clear my throat and tip my chin up. "I need to see it."

He tucks his phone into his pocket then climbs through his window and over to mine. I stand and move over to the bed, and he slides in next to me.

"Are you sure you want to see it?" he asks.

I nod, and he pulls his phone out of his pocket. He unlocks it, opens the app, and hands it over.

I stare at the profile. Sure enough, it's a photo of me from the office Christmas party two years ago. The details are right, but as I glance through the videos posted, it's not me.

"I don't know Stephanie's body all that well, but it could be her. Don't you think?" I ask.

He shrugs. "I haven't paid her much attention, to be honest."

I twist my lips, and I click one of the previews. There's no talking, just swaying to some quiet music in the background. She mostly fills the screen, but I look wildly around the room for any clue. I come up empty. The walls are white and empty, like maybe she took down some photos to record this video.

She slides her fingers into the top of her panties, and a notification pops up on the screen.

Want to see more?

I click the *yes* button, and it takes me to another screen for payment information. I glance at Tristan, who's chewing his bottom lip, and he nods. I click accept, and it takes me back to the video.

There's still no face, but she turns around and plays with her hair a little, pulling it up like she's making a ponytail before letting it drop.

"Wait," Tristan says. "Can you rewind that?"

My brows dip, and I click the screen. A video control bar pops up, and I click the rewind button.

"Pause it," he says. I click pause.

"What are you looking at?" I ask.

"Right there," he says. He takes the phone from my hand and moves the video bar just slightly as she pulls her hair up. "There's a tattoo on her neck just under her hairline."

He moves the video around just a little again, but it's impossible to make out what it is. I spot just the edge of some ink, but it's blurred and hard to see.

"Does Stephanie have a tattoo?" he asks.

I shrug. "I have no idea. I've never seen her with her hair up."

He blows out a breath. "It's not much, but it's a lead. We can watch more of these and see if we can get a clear view of it, or we could file a police report and let them do the research."

He clicks play, and we watch as she unhooks her bra, the camera taking in her naked back. She crosses her arms and turns around, then makes a big show of lowering one arm at a time so we can get a good view of her boobs.

She plays with them, and I roll my eyes as I fast forward. But there aren't any more shots of her neck.

"Let's file the report tomorrow," I say, and he nods as I hand him back his phone.

He scrolls down a little, and he tries another video. There's no neck in this one, either. He tries a few more, and he glances over at me.

I shrug. "Try one more, and then we'll let the police handle the rest."

He clicks it, and it's a lot like the last one. It's like she filmed a hundred clips of herself doing the same thing over and over.

No neck in this one, either.

No other clues.

"Are you okay?" he asks as he put his phone back in his pocket.

"Yeah, I'm all right. Just the thought that this is out there, that someone somewhere might really believe this is me…it's gross," I say, and my stomach twists at the thought. "In one way, I feel a little violated."

"You have every right to feel that way. What this person is doing…it has to be illegal, right? We'll get to the bottom of it," he says.

We're both quiet a few beats, and then I glance over at him. "Is it always going to be like this?"

He reaches over and squeezes my hand. "I don't know," he says, and his honesty makes my chest tighten with fear. "But I've got your back, Tess. T and T, always, okay?"

"Always," I repeat.

I fall asleep in his arms, and he's gone when I wake up in the morning. I meet him at the new house after a shower and breakfast, and there's already a huge delivery truck waiting out front.

"Where do you want the couch?" one of the delivery workers asks me as I walk in.

"Is it the sectional or the sofa and loveseat?" I ask.

"Sofa," he says.

"Over there," I say, pointing toward the middle of the front room. The furniture is arriving at our new house today, and we're moving in next Monday—just as soon as Tristan gets back from minicamp this weekend. We're both excited, but we're both intent on not rushing things, too. I *can't* rush things anyway right now, not in my current state of carrying this watermelon in my stomach.

I walk through the house and into the kitchen, where I spot Tristan talking to Walter Keegan.

"Any other details you'd like to provide?" Walt asks.

Tristan shakes his head.

It's so strange seeing Walter Keegan in a police uniform. He was always a nice kid, but I remember him jumping a fence to get drunk out in the cornfields behind town when I was a freshman and he was a senior. Funny how he's the one trying to stop kids from doing the same things he used to do as he works to uphold the law.

"I think that's everything," Tristan says.

Walt nods and glances at me. "Tristan filled me in on the impersonator. I'll share the information with Roger, and we'll get to work on it."

There isn't a lot of crime in the small town of Fallon Ridge, and we share our officers with the town next to us. The small police department is made up of the police chief, two sergeants, and four officers—one of which is Roger, the town's detective.

"Have a great day, ma'am. We'll be in touch with any questions," Walt says to me, and he heads through the house and out the front door.

"You filed the report already?" I ask softly.

Tristan nods as his eyes fall tenderly to me. "I didn't want you to have to relive it again."

I practically fall into his arms. "You're so good to me."

He sighs. "Doing my best," he finally says. "And I have some good news, if you'd like it."

"I'd love some good news."

"Richard emailed me this morning," he says, referring to his lawyer.

"He did?" My heart thunders in my chest as anxiety pours through my body and into my words. He said it's good news, so it has to be what I'm praying it'll be…right?

He nods, and his lips lift. "Cameron signed the papers."

"He did?" I ask again, but this time my voice holds relief.

He presses a soft kiss to my lips. "He did," he confirms.

"The sectional?" one of the delivery workers yells through the house, interrupting our intimate moment.

"In here," I yell back, indicating the family room on the other side of the kitchen.

Our day transitions from whatever weirdness is happening on a porn site over to making sure all our new furniture ends up in the right place as Tristan goes upstairs to direct the delivery men up there. I stay downstairs to place everything down here.

I'm sure we'll have a chance to talk more later, but for now, at least one fire is out. Now for the rest of them.

CHAPTER 9

Tessa

Later never comes as the house keeps us occupied the majority of the day. We go to his parents' house for dinner—with my mother, too—and then he has to pack for minicamp. He decided to leave tonight and get a hotel in Chicago for his early morning flight, so we're saying hasty goodbyes before he heads out the door.

"Come with me," he says softly.

I glance down at my stomach. "You know I wish I could, but the doctor said I shouldn't fly after twenty-eight weeks due to the placenta issue." I'm over twenty-nine weeks now, so we're in that zone. "Besides, you'll be busy all weekend."

"You're right," he says. He zips up his duffel bag and pulls me into his arms. "I love you." He embraces me tightly, warmly, and he backs up to press a gentle kiss to my lips. He backs away, and he kneels to the ground. He rests both hands over my stomach. "And I love you, too." He presses a kiss there, and heat presses behind my eyes.

I'll never get over how much he loves us both, how he's *there* for us both when I thought we'd never even see each other again.

"We love you, too," I say, and the heat spills over my lashes and onto my cheeks. I swipe at the tears. "We'll miss you."

He kisses me again. "I'll miss you, too. I'll be back late Sunday night. Just please, please be here when I get home. Keep your phone out of toilets, and try to get off pelvic rest by then."

I giggle. "I promise. And hopefully I'll be released from rest at my appointment on Tuesday." I squirm a little. "Though if I do something deserving of punishment..." I trail off.

His eyes heat as he brands me to the spot where I stand. "Want more already?"

I lift a shoulder. "It was...different. *Hot* different. *Good* different."

His eyes flash with hunger. "Then you better behave yourself." He shrugs and winks. "Or don't."

I think I might choose option two.

And on that note, after he takes off, I head home and open up Instagram. I check Stephanie's account and scroll through, looking for any signs at all of a tattoo. I don't see any.

I pull open her contact on my text messages. I don't know how quickly the Fallon Ridge Police Department works, but maybe I can work faster.

Me: *Are you free for lunch this weekend?*

It's probably a terrible idea, but I hit the send button before I can stop myself.

She writes back nearly immediately.

Stephanie: *Yes! Would love to see you. Could use some craft fair ideas. Tomorrow at noon? There's a diner in Geneseo, midway for both of us, or I could come to you.*

Me: *Geneseo sounds good. See you then.*

I'm certain Tristan's going to punish me for this idea...and I'm sort of relishing the thought of it.

I catch my mom in the kitchen before she leaves for work the next morning.

"You're up early," she says.

"Couldn't get comfortable," I admit.

She kisses my cheek. "Can I make you something for breakfast?"

I shake my head. "I don't want to interrupt your schedule. But do you want to go to Davenport tonight to shop for the baby? I want to get decorations for the nursery, and they have some baby stores I want to look at."

"Of course," she says. "I'd love to."

"I also wanted to mention that I'm meeting Stephanie for lunch today," I blurt. I guess I don't want to go meet her without *somebody* knowing.

"You are?" she asks, her tone surprised.

I shrug, playing it off because I'm not ready to tell her what I think she might be doing until I have some solid evidence. "She's planning a craft fair for her town, and I thought it might be nice to offer some feedback about how ours went."

"That's so nice of you," she says.

We make small talk before she heads to work. I take my time with breakfast and showering, and then it's time to meet Stephanie.

I find myself nervous as I navigate toward Geneseo, and when I pull into the parking lot, I immediately spot her car.

She's already inside, waiting at a table for me even though I'm five minutes early.

I spot her immediately, and I try to reconcile whether the girl in the video is the same girl sitting at the table. It's hard to tell, but what I could see of the ends of her hair looks the same. I guess the same could be said for lots of women, though, and it's possible the girl in the video wore a wig or used filters.

She waves me down with both arms like I can't see her, and I'm disappointed that she chose a booth rather than a table with chairs. How the hell am I supposed to get a look at her neck when she's got a tall booth behind her?

I'll find a way, and it hits me like a bolt of lightning as I approach the table. I dramatically rub my pregnant stomach. "Thanks for grabbing a table. I'm so sorry, but would you mind if we sit in chairs instead of a booth? Sliding in is getting harder and harder."

"Oh, of course," she says, and she taps her forehead. "Silly me. I didn't even think about that!"

"It's no problem." I offer a wide smile, and we call the hostess over to reseat us.

I follow behind her, staring at her neck, and I guess I'm following a bit too closely because she stops suddenly, and I bump right into her on accident.

I push her hair to the side as I do it, trying to get a glimpse under her hair as I take advantage of my proximity. No dice. I can't see a thing.

"Sorry," I mumble when she turns back to give me a look for bumping into her.

"It's okay," she says with a smile.

I stare at my menu once we're seated. How the hell am I going to get her to show me her neck?

I think about going to the bathroom and just sweeping her hair to the side when I get back then playing it off as a friendly gesture, but I've barely acknowledged her existence in the time I've known her. We're not at that level of friendliness. I don't know if I'm at that level of friendliness with *any* of my friends, now that I think about it. When was the last time I played with Sara's hair?

Never.

The answer is never.

I haven't played with another woman's hair since…well, maybe ever.

I order a burger and fries because baby girl is hungry.

"That sounds delicious," she tells the server. "I'll have the same."

"What have you been up to?" I ask, shifting into small talk.

She practically preens under my question, like all she's ever wanted was for me to show some interest.

I'm getting highly weird vibes here, but maybe it's just because I'm hungry.

"Working on the craft fair. How'd you get so many vendors?" she asks. She leans in. "Did you have to pay a lot of money for them?"

I shake my head. "Most donated their services."

Her brows dip. "How?"

"Tristan," I say. "The vendors knew with him involved, they'd be getting tons of press coverage. And they weren't wrong." I lift a shoulder, and her face sours a bit.

"Of course," she mutters.

"Excuse me?" I ask.

She purses her lips. "You've got it so easy, that's all. An NFL boyfriend to help coax along your little fair? Makes things a little simpler, you know?"

I resist the urge to tell her she knows nothing about me and that it actually *hasn't* been all that easy. But I don't know what she's going through, and I'm a little afraid I'll just set her off.

"I could talk to him and see if he could help sponsor your event, too," I say, mostly as a way to ward off more questions about Tristan. He won't be interested in helping her, particularly not if our suspicions about her are correct, but if it shifts us to a new topic of conversation where I can work in a way to get a look at her neck, I'll say just about anything right now.

Her eyes light up, and I'm not convinced he was right when he said she's more interested in me than in him. "You'd do that?"

"Of course," I say, reaching over and patting her hand across the table.

Her eyes move to where our hands connect, and she eyes that connection for a beat.

The strange vibe surrounding us seems to intensify, and when her eyes lift to mine, I see something there—something a little terrifying.

I pull my hand away quickly and busy it by picking up the little sandwich board on the table advertising the specials while I pretend to study it.

"You've really just got it all, don't you?" she murmurs. "The rich, athletic, hot boyfriend, the baby, the father…"

I don't know if she means the father of the baby or *our* father, but I don't ask, and further, I'm not sure she meant for me to hear it at all, if she meant to say it aloud.

I sit silently, my brows knit together with my eyes still down on the specials as I wait for her to finish her thought, but she never does. When I glance up, she's studying me. She knits her brows together the way I'm doing. I tuck some hair behind my ear after I set down the specials probably out of some nervous habit, and she does the same.

She seems to be mirroring the way I'm sitting. She looks at how I'm folding my hands, and she mimics it.

Is she…trying to *be* me?

I get her wanting the things I have. Despite the rather rough events I've made it through, I'm in a place where I find myself quite blessed.

I set a hand on my stomach out of habit. I'm suddenly scared, and I guess it's mother's instinct to protect the baby.

She sets her hand on her stomach, too.

She's not pregnant, and she sets her hand on her stomach.

This is getting weirder and weirder.

No MISTAKE

I shouldn't have come. I should be at home resting, waiting for Tristan to get back from minicamp, and instead I'm crafting one hell of a reason for him to punish me when he gets back.

But I still need to see if she has a tattoo on the back of her neck. I can't leave here without accomplishing my mission.

"Excuse me," I say. "I need to use the restroom." It's a lie. I don't need to use the restroom, but I do need a minute to text my mom to help get me out of this.

"I'll come, too."

Great.

Alone in a small room with a crazy person who wants to be me.

Scared is an understatement.

I smile and stand, and I hold out a hand. Maybe I can use this to my advantage. "After you."

I follow her and watch her hair sway as she moves, but it never moves enough to see if there's a tattoo under there.

I lock myself in a stall and force myself to take care of business, and I slip my phone out of my purse.

I shoot off a quick text to my mom.

Me: *Text me with a reason to leave lunch in fifteen minutes please. Don't ask why, will explain later.*

I send it and delete it immediately as a just in case, and then I flush and exit the stall to wash my hands.

She's already at the sink, and after I finish drying my hands, I get another idea. I reach into my purse and pull out a hair tie. If she wants to be like me…if she wants to mimic my every move…then maybe she'll do what I'm doing and I can peep her neck.

I pull my hair up into a ponytail and fan myself. "It's hot in here, right?"

Her brows draw together as she tilts her head. "Not really. Must be the pregnancy."

She heads out of the bathroom first.

Damn.

Of all the times to *stop* doing everything I'm doing, this is the one she chooses.

Our burgers are being served as we walk back to the table, and I dig right in. I finish in record time, still trying to come up with some way to get a view of that tattoo, but I can't think of any other way to do it.

"Do you have any tattoos?" I blurt. I pop a fry into my mouth as my cheeks redden.

Her eyes narrow at me. "A few. Do you?"

I shake my head. Why the hell did I just blurt that out? "No, but I was thinking of getting one. Do they hurt?"

"What do you want to get?" she asks rather than answering my question.

"I'm not sure. Maybe a butterfly."

"Everyone has butterflies," she murmurs.

"What do you have?" I ask.

She narrows her eyes at me. "Why are you asking?"

I shrug, trying to keep it light as I play off my real motivation here. "Just curious. I was thinking about getting it on my wrist. Do you think that would hurt?"

"I've heard the wrist is less painful than, say, the ribs," she says.

Ribs? The girl in the video didn't have a rib tattoo. "Do you have a rib tattoo?" I ask.

She nods. "It was super painful."

Maybe she covered it with make-up or a filter or something.

"Where else do you have them?" I press, trying to get an answer to my question. Just then a text from my mom comes through.

Mom: *I need your help at the church. Molly didn't show up to teach her religion class. Can you come fill in?*

"Oh no," I say, the frustration in my voice real as I felt like I was finally getting somewhere. I can't just ignore this, though. I have to keep playing the game.

"What?" Her eyes are wide with concern.

"My mom needs my help at the church. I better head out," I say, pulling a twenty out of my wallet. It's way more than my burger cost, but I really do just want to get out of here despite not being any closer to an answer.

"But we've barely even talked about the craft fair," she protests.

"Right, well—I'll talk to Tristan and get back to you, okay?" I say as I stand.

She huffs out a disappointed *fine*, and she stands to give me a hug.

"I'm so sorry," I say, really trying to hit the apologetic angle. I am sorry—sorry that this lunch was such a freaking bust and that I just keep getting more and more weirded out by this woman.

I try to get a peek at her neck as I hug her, but I'm at the wrong angle.

I don't see anything there, but I also didn't get a good look, and her hair was blocking the majority of my view anyway.

I take the hell off before she can stop me.

I call my mom on the way back to Fallon Ridge.

"Do you really need me to come in?" I ask.

"No, honey, I just said that to help you out. What's going on with you?"

My voice trembles a little as I start to recount all the things I haven't told her yet. First the Instagram photos, then the craft fair and the nursing program, the JustFans profile, and finally, how strange she was acting at lunch.

"It sounds like she's got an obsession with you," she says. "Or possibly Tristan. I think you should just stay far, far away."

"I know I should, but I also want her to stop. Maybe if I try to reason with her…" I trail off as I think that part through.

She sighs. "I know, Tessi-cat, and I don't blame you for wanting to be nice. But think on this, too. You're engaged to a football superstar. Millions of women want him, maybe your half-sister included…but he wants you. Protect that with everything you've got, baby girl."

"You're right," I say, and I think she means to share that as a good thing. I take it a different way, though. "But I think what that means is that I'm going to be the target for a whole lot of hatred."

I guess the question now is whether I buck up and get used to it as I hold Tristan's hand through it…or whether it's enough to scare me away for good.

CHAPTER 10

Tristan

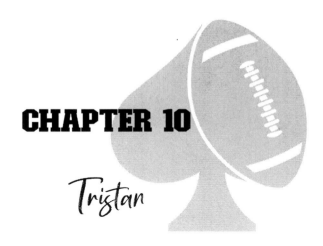

Camp doesn't start until tomorrow, but I'm in town a day early. Travis invited me to stay at his place in his guest room, and that means we have the rest of the day to relax before we have to be at our first practice early tomorrow morning.

But *relax* means different things to different people. Travis said he'd have a few guys over, and it has turned into a party with the regular Thursday Night Crew.

"Coax tonight?" Cory asks me on the down low away from Deon and Patrick, who still don't know about the members-only club.

I laugh. "As Travis said to me not so long ago, it's probably not a good idea for me to go given the fact that I'm engaged to another woman and she's expecting our baby."

He shrugs. "Marriage didn't stop you before."

"That was different," I argue, but it's a feeble argument given the fact that he's right. If anybody outside of my tight circle of friends knew about the third level of the exclusive club while I was still married to another woman, I'm certain judgements would be cast.

But they'd be cast no matter what I choose to do with my life. I can't stop living just because people might not agree with every decision I make.

"How?" he asks.

"For one thing, it was a sham of a marriage I was being forced to stay in," I point out.

"I'm sure that's how outsiders would see it, too." He moves onto Jaxon to ask him next, confirming my thoughts about what others might think.

It doesn't matter, though. I'm in a good place now, and I'm not going to risk that by going somewhere I don't even want Tessa to know about.

Travis declines since the party's at his place, but as Cory and Jaxon make their way toward the door early, Patrick calls out to them. "Where are you two assholes going?"

They exchange a glance, and then Jaxon turns around to face him. "A sex club." He says it in that way where you can't tell whether he's joking or not, and silence falls over the room before he bursts out laughing.

Travis's wide eyes meet mine, and I'm not exactly sure how to react, so I just start laughing, too.

"You're such a fucking clown," I say as they head out the door still howling with laughter.

"Where are they really going?" Patrick presses, and I just shrug and tip my beer bottle to my lips.

Travis changes the subject, and an hour or so later, Deon calls it a night first. Patrick talks Austin into going to Honeys, and Travis talks me into a bar nearby.

It's late in Iowa, but I send a text to Tessa anyway before we head out.

Me: *How was your day?*

Her reply comes quickly.

Tessa: *It was a little strange.*

Me: *Everything okay?*

My phone rings a few seconds later.

"Hey," I answer.

"Hey. Yeah, everything's fine. I, uh…I think I did something worthy of one of your punishments."

I chuckle even as I think about where I learned those particular techniques. "Did you purposely do something worthy or was it an accident?"

"I texted Stephanie to see if she wanted to go to lunch with me today. I wanted to see if she has a tattoo on her neck," she admits.

"And?"

"I couldn't tell, and she was being super weird," she says.

"Has she ever been *normal*?" I ask.

"No, but she was like…I don't know. Maybe I was imagining it."

"What?" I press.

"She was imitating everything I was doing. If I tucked my hair behind my ear, she did it too. If I picked up my water, so did she. She followed me to the bathroom when I told her I had to go but I was really just trying to get away to tell my mom to text me an emergency so I could get the hell out of there."

"Tess…I think you should stay away from her. It sounds like some weird *Fatal Attraction* type shit going on there and I don't want you to get hurt," I warn quietly.

She sighs. "You're right. But what do I do if she just shows up uninvited?"

"You shut the door in her face," I say thickly.

"You ready?" Travis calls from the other room. "Our ride's here!"

"I need to run." I sigh. I don't really want to get off the phone with her. She seems to feel a certain way about what went down today, and I want to allow her the space to talk about it…but Travis is waiting for me. "I'm heading out with a buddy, but get some sleep, and I'll talk to you tomorrow, okay?"

"Be safe. I love you," she says.

"I love you, too." I hang up, and I meet Travis by the door.

"Everything okay?" he asks.

I nod, and we get into the Lyft he ordered. We're dropped at O'Leary's, a bar not too far from Travis's place. It tends to be a hangout for players who want to avoid the nightclub scene, but tonight I don't see any of our friends from the team. We shouldn't be out, either, considering we have an early morning, but we're not here to get fucked up—just to have a drink or two before we call it a night.

The booths are all taken, so we sit at the bar. Both Travis and I wear ballcaps pulled down low in an attempt to be discreet, but Travis has tattoos on his arms that make him instantly recognizable—and instantly hotter to women, by the way.

We've barely toasted to our first sip when a woman slips between us to talk to Travis. The music's loud, but not loud enough that I can't hear every word she says. "What are you doing here instead of Coax?"

"I could ask you the same," he answers. "I hardly recognized you in jeans and a t-shirt."

She laughs. "I like to *dress up* for the club."

"And I like to grab a drink with my buddy once in a while," he says, nodding toward me.

She turns to look at me. "Tristan," she says, her eyes lighting up. I vaguely recognize her, but like the time I saw Brandi outside of the club, it's harder to place the women I've seen there.

"Brandi's meeting me here later," she says, and I don't like the way she says it like I stake some ownership over Brandi, like we're somehow more than friends when we're not. I took care of her a few times, and we had a friendship inside Coax. That's it.

At least…that's all it is for me. I can't say the same about Brandi.

"Tell her I said hi," I say with a press of my lips and a nod, hoping it's enough of a hint to let her know I'm not interested in anything other than being friendly.

"I'm sure she'd love to tell you herself," she says, and she winks. A new song starts playing, and she gasps. "Oh! It's my song!" She runs to the dance floor with her group of friends, most of which I don't recognize, and I can't help but wonder whether they know about Coax. I recognize Sapphire, the girl who Troy Bodine *punished* my second night there. But she's the only one who looks familiar, so I'm guessing they either aren't local celebrities or they aren't members. Or maybe it's the fact that I haven't been there in a long time, so I've lost sight of who's who anymore.

"What's her name?" I ask, trying to make conversation.

"Mackenzie," he says. "She's a good girl." He winks, and I wonder what, exactly, he's done with her.

It's not my business, but running into her here and Brandi at the Big D Bash just tells me what a small world it really is—or what a small network of local celebrities Vegas proves to be.

Or what a big network Coax actually is.

I'm reminded of that moments later when Troy Bodine interrupts my conversation with Travis.

Now *him* I recognize outside of the club, and I guess it shouldn't come as a surprise since Sapphire's here.

He slides in between us and tosses one arm around my shoulder and the other around Travis's. The man has a large wingspan, and he wears a suit in a jeans kind of place. He's imposing and a little intimidating and what he did to Sapphire for punishment still weighs on my mind.

Actually, I guess except for withholding aftercare, it's similar to what I did to Tessa for punishment not so long ago. I may have picked up a trick or two from watching him.

Does that make Troy my mentor?

I nearly laugh aloud at the thought.

"I'm holding a charity event mid-May, and I would love to see you both there," he says. He leans in and lowers his voice a little. "I always offer spots to members first."

Travis glances at me. "I'll be around, but this asshole is vacationing in the Midwest."

I chuckle. I wouldn't exactly call it a vacation, but sure. "I'll be around mid-May for OTAs. When's the event?"

"Saturday the fourteenth," he says, and he nods at the bartender. Just like that, the bartender gets to work on his drink, and I realize how goddamn powerful this guy is.

He's not just a former baseball player. He's part-owner of a club built for people with money, he's got a shit ton of money, and he's got women eager to get on their knees just for the chance to suck him off. He's still involved with the game, too, but I don't study his career enough to know in what capacity.

"That's OTA weekend," Travis says.

"Then it's settled. I'll have my secretary send you the formal invitation, but I will see you both there. Bring a date," Troy says, and then he walks away—not even giving me a chance to decline or explain that my future wife probably shouldn't be boarding a plane so close to her due date.

I guess I'm going to a charity event on May fourteenth…an event run by a sex club owner who demanded I bring a date.

CHAPTER 11

Tessa

"What are you doing here?" I ask, my jaw slightly open as I stare at my best friend where she stands on my mom's front porch.

"Surprise!" she says, and she giggles. "I'm here to see this new house this football player of yours bought for you."

I giggle. "Come on in," I say, and I open the door wider to my mom's house. I'm currently taking a break from the new house. I've been back and forth most of the morning, dropping things off so I'm ready for Tristan when he gets back home tomorrow, and my mom shooed me out after the last trip, telling me I had to rest.

She's right. I'm supposed to be resting, not running back and forth moving into a new home.

So I've been sitting on the couch for the last hour, doing exactly as she said. I watched Sara's car pull up in front of my mom's house, and I went to the door immediately as I watched her get out of the car and walk up the driveway.

"I'm just so happy you're here," I say, pulling her into a hug.

"That's two weekends in a row with your bestie," she says with a flip of her hair, and I giggle. "So first, let's catch up. Tell me all the things."

"Not much new since I saw you last weekend," I admit. "But I did get my new phone working." I grin as I hold it up to show it off.

"Maybe consider memorizing your password in case it ever happens again. And maybe a phone number or two."

I giggle. "Sage advice."

"Where's the boy? Do I get to meet him?" she asks.

I shake my head. "Sorry, babe. He's in Vegas for team stuff. They have these off-season workouts that aren't technically mandatory, but's definitely expected to be there."

She twists her lips. "Another time then."

I nod. "Ready to go see the house?"

"Can I use your restroom first? And I hate to bother you, but could I get some water before we go?"

"Of course," I say. "Excuse me for being a terrible hostess and not offering those things. I'm just so surprised you're here in the best way."

She grins. "Me too, girl. Me too."

I point down the hall to where the restroom is, and I grab a bottle of water from the fridge. I set out a plate with some cheese, grapes, and crackers on it, too, and when she comes out, she sits across from me at the table.

"Have you thought about when you two are getting married?" she asks, nodding down to the ring sparkling on my hand.

I lift a shoulder. "We don't have a date set in stone. At first I thought I wanted to wait until the baby got here, but I'm not so sure anymore."

Her brows dip. "What are you thinking?"

"Maybe before then," I admit.

She gasps a little. "Before then? But isn't the baby due in like…"

"Less than two months?" I fill in for her, and then I nod. "Yeah."

"Why so fast?"

"I want to be his wife," I say softly. "It's everything I wanted since I was twelve."

"Right." She nods like she already knows that. "And you've waited this long. So why the rush?"

I blow out a breath. There are a lot of reasons I want to do it sooner than later.

For one thing, I want Tristan's dad to be there. It's important to him, and it's important to me.

I haven't mentioned Russ's illness to Sara, though, and it's not my story to tell.

But it's not just that. I'm anxious about the spotlight, and I don't want our big day splashed all over the media because of who he is. I want it to be intimate and special and just for the two of us. And what better way to achieve that than to do it in nearly total secrecy?

But I don't mention that, either. Instead, I set my hand on my stomach and allow her to draw her own conclusions. I glance over at her meaningfully, and her eyes widen a little as understanding dawns.

"You're protecting yourself and the baby," she murmurs.

"A stable home with two loving parents versus a broken home where the doctor is cheating on his wife? Seems like Tristan and I would have the advantage there."

"You would," she agrees.

I reach across the table and grab her hand. "I want you there. I want you to be my maid of honor."

Tears glisten in her eyes at my words. "I would love to be, Tessa." We're both quiet a beat, and then she says, "Here?"

I shrug. "I'm thinking Vegas, as long as my doctor clears it. You up for a little trip?"

She giggles. "I've never been there."

"Me neither, but I'm moving there in a few months, so time to get acquainted."

"I'm in for whatever you need from me, girlfriend." She pauses, and then she narrows her eyes at me. "Wait a minute. Does this mean you're getting married before me?"

I shrug. "I mean…I have to talk to Tristan first, but it's looking that way, isn't it?"

She shakes her head with wonder. "I can't get over it. I'm just so freaking happy for you. At Christmas I was so worried about you. You were devastated after what Cam did to you, and rightly so. I swear I glare at him every time I see him in the office, by the way. And now you're getting everything you deserved. You're getting your happy ending."

She stands and I do, too, as she pulls me up and hugs me.

"Love you, my friend," I murmur into our embrace.

"I love you, too, and I'm so happy for you." She squeezes me once more before she lets me go. "Now go get your cute little butt changed so you can take me on a tour of this house your boy bought you."

I grin. It sounds so weird hearing her describe it that way, but this is reality, and I couldn't be happier.

CHAPTER 12

Tessa

"I picture lilac bushes along here." I point as we walk up the sidewalk toward my red front door. "And Tristan's house had rhododendron bushes, so maybe some of those out back. And I've always wanted one of those little flower border things where I could plant annuals every year. Maybe a garden out back," I say as I unlock the front door.

"This is gorgeous," she says, her eyes on the house.

I nod toward an empty spot on the porch to my left. "I ordered a porch swing, too. Can you just imagine sitting there, gazing downtown or dreaming about the future while the baby naps?" I turn the doorknob, and the second I open the door, the loud greeting shocks the hell out of me.

"Surprise!"

I fall back a little, but Sara's there to catch me.

"Happy baby shower!" she says, and I turn toward her with narrowed eyes.

"You knew about this?"

"Girl, I *planned* this. With your mom, of course," she says, and my mom comes running up to us first. She envelopes me in a hug, and she grabs onto Sara next.

Sue is right behind my mom, and behind her is everyone else from town. Mrs. Beatty, Mrs. Burton, Mrs. Sullivan, and

Mrs. Cleary are the first in the line-up. Their endless support for the Fallon Festival was incredible, and now they're here supporting me again.

Mrs. Asher is here, and several other Fallon Ridge teachers my mom is friendly with, too. All the ladies from the auxiliary club are here, and even Mayor Hanson's wife showed up.

I spot several girls from my class who are still in town—or close enough to show up to any of Fallon Ridge's events. Lauren, Kristen, Wendy, Nicole, Jamie, Jen, and, of course, Tiffany all made it to the party. Most of their moms are here, too, a byproduct of living in a small town. The invitations to an event like this end up more political than anything else.

I haven't spoken to most of the girls I attended high school with since the craft fair—and some not since my father's funeral.

We're not friends the way we once were anymore. In fact, I don't know if I could *ever* really count any of them among my friends. They were friendly with me because I was close to Tristan. He was who they wanted, and I would venture to guess that's part of why they're here today.

That…plus, I suspect many of them showed up today out of an obligation to seeing what gossip they could drum up rather than actually caring about me.

I push those thoughts aside. Whatever the reason is, they're here today, and I'm glad they came.

And then I spot two figures toward the back of the room off by themselves, and a strange shiver crawls up my spine.

My half-sister Stephanie and Auntie Jane.

What the hell are they doing here?

Either of them?

I would *never* have invited Stephanie to anything personal, and Auntie Jane is the last person I'd want to celebrate another baby out of wedlock with.

No MISTAKE

But they're both here, and it's weird that they're talking to each other.

I guess she's Stephanie's aunt, too, and I'm curious as to whether they've spoken before. Maybe at Dad's funeral, but I don't recall seeing them together. It was a busy day, though. I saw Tristan for the first time in seven years. Cam showed up. My father had died and I met two of my half-siblings.

To say I was distracted that day would be a gross understatement.

It's weird seeing her here in my new home. She looks a lot like my father, only older and female, and she acted much like him, too.

Except I never knew my father at all, apparently.

I choose not to focus on that today. Instead, I focus on what an amazing gift I've been given.

My mom and Sara went all out with this perfect baby shower. We eat pink cupcakes, we play games, we eat finger foods and appetizers, we play more games, I open gifts, and there's plenty of laughter and merriment.

Mrs. Burton made the baby a quilt, and Coach Beatty's mother knitted a winter hat and scarves. Margaret made some kid-friendly soaps as well as some special bath bombs for me when I'm up to baths. The girls from high school all chipped in to get the dream baby stroller I wanted. I hadn't planned on registering, but my mom suggested it a while ago since she said people in town would want to buy us gifts.

She was right.

I can't think of a single thing on that list we *didn't* get today, and my mom informs me halfway through the shower that she picked our new house as the setting for the surprise shower so we wouldn't have to haul all the gifts from some other location back to the house.

I can't help but think that was a pretty brilliant plan as I glance at the presents piled up all around me once I've finished opening them.

Sara takes meticulous notes so I can write out thank you cards, and eventually the guests start to leave.

Before she leaves, though, I spot Tiffany talking with my aunt. The hairs on the back of my neck stand on end. Does Tiffany know that's the aunt I stayed with when I left town?

Is she asking all the right questions…and is Auntie Jane *answering* them?

Exhaustion hits me as the surprise mixes with the activity of the day. I flop onto the couch as my mom shuts the door behind Coach Beatty's mother, and all that's left is my mom, Tristan's mom, Sara, Stephanie, and Auntie Jane.

Auntie Jane had to have driven in from Chicago. I haven't spoken to her other than a cursory and polite greeting when I first saw her, and I also haven't spoken much to Stephanie today.

They're hanging back like they're part of the family, and I guess in the technical sense they are.

But Auntie Jane knows my secret.

She's one of the few who does, and I know she'd be discreet, but I still can't help feel a certain way when I see her talking the entire day with the half-sister produced from one of my father's affairs.

"What an incredible day," I say. Stephanie and Auntie Jane are in the kitchen, and I'm on the living room couch with my mom, Sue, and Sara nearby. "Thank you all so much for this wonderful surprise."

"It was all Janet," Sue says. "She's been planning this for months now."

Sara nods. "She has. She asked me for opinions, but it was all her."

I sit up and squeeze my mom's hands. "Thanks, Mama."

"Anything for my little girl," she says.

"You need any help cleaning up?" Sue asks. She glances around, and the place is as meticulously neat as it was before the party, because that's the kind of person Sue is. She already washed all the dishes, cleaned up the wrapping paper, and broke down boxes. Sara and my mom carried most of the gifts up to the nursery.

"You've done so much," my mom says to her. "I can't thank you enough."

"That's our grandbaby, too," she says, hugging my mom. "I'm happy to do whatever I can."

Tears spring to my eyes, and Sara leans over and tosses her arm around me as my mom walks Sue out. "Congratulations, Mama," she says to me. "You scored big with that Tristan guy and his family."

She's damn right about that.

Stephanie takes off next, and then Sara takes off on her drive back to Chicago.

Soon it's just my mom, me…and Auntie Jane.

I feel awkward with her here.

She reminds me of some of the worst moments of my life. She was civil enough to me, and she took care of my basic needs, but she was neither loving nor warm toward me when I stayed with her. Instead, that entire period of my life feels like one big punishment.

I don't hate her, per se, but I can't say I really like her, either.

"I need to get on the road, too, but I waited for everyone else to leave so I could talk with you both," she says.

I suck in a breath.

"I just want to say I'm so happy the way things have worked out for you, Tessa. Things were difficult not so long ago, but it appears you've rebounded beautifully." Not a hint of merriment is in her eyes despite her words, and yet again, she reminds me of her brother. He was never very merry, either.

Still, I'm a little surprised that she's being as nice as she is. I'm a little surprised she showed up. I know how she feels about premarital sex. I know how she feels about babies born to single mothers.

And yet...she's here.

"Thank you, Auntie Jane," I say softly.

Questions play in the recesses of my mind.

Does she know what happened to the baby?

Did she ever get to hold him?

Does she know where he is now?

She wouldn't. Those records were sealed.

Still...I can't help but wonder. I can't help but wonder whether there's some way to unlock those mysteries, to find answers to questions I first asked seven years ago.

Just as I'm about to open my mouth to ask, she says, "I've spoken with both Stephanie and Michael. Stephanie could use a friend, I think. Michael is well-adjusted. I thought I would mention that to you."

Is this her way of telling me I need to befriend my half-sister?

Because if it is...I'm not sure I can do that. Not when I think she's the one dancing naked pretending to me be on JustFans. Not when I don't trust her.

Not when I'm a little scared of her.

I'm a little scared of Auntie Jane, too, if I'm being totally honest.

We say our goodbyes without another chance for me to ask any of the questions plaguing my mind, and then it's just my mom and me.

"This was incredible, Mama. Really. Thank you so much," I say, drawing her into a hug.

No **MISTAKE**

She squeezes me back. "It was fun planning it. I'm just so excited to meet that sweet baby girl."

"Me too." We withdraw from our embrace and head over to the couch. "Can I ask you a question?"

She nods as we both sit.

"Stephanie and Auntie Jane?"

She laughs and shrugs. "I knew *not* inviting them would spark even more town gossip."

She's probably right about that.

Still, the thought that Tiffany Gable was over there talking to her sends a chill up my spine.

CHAPTER 13

Tristan

I spent the morning testing footwork techniques with the other wide receivers at practice while we polished up on the playbook. It's our first practice with this year's playbook, and everybody prepares for the upcoming season in different ways. The players' association makes sure nothing is mandatory, but it's still the team's expectation to be here. So when I glance around and see nearly all the veteran players present, I'm not surprised.

Minicamp is much lower-key than training camp. We have meetings and training sessions, and it's a nice reminder as we'll get back to two-a-days come August.

It comes mid-off-season to force us back into the mindset, and it falls two weeks before I find out for sure whether the team will be exercising my fifth-year option, which means even though most of the guys are moving at half-speed, I don't have that luxury.

Thanks to the treadmill in my parents' garage and the daily workouts, I'm in decent shape...but I still find myself gasping for air as we run some drills.

I need to get back into it, but I have over three months before training camp begins. I have plenty of time.

Except there's a baby on the way, and maybe a wedding—a talk that keeps getting pushed back. There are secrets I'm trying to keep and a history I want to forget.

There are people trying to come between us, whether it's Savannah or Stephanie or whoever texted me about Coax. That will never change, and I've still got the fear that she's going to bail on me. I'm terrified she'll decide it's all too much and walk away.

It happened once. What if it happens again?

I've invested everything into her. She owns my entire soul, and that means she has the power to destroy it. To destroy *me*.

"Whoa, Higs," Coach Jeff says as I plow through the line of men in front of me to practice a slant route. "These are supposed to be non-contact practices." He pulls me aside. "What's going on?"

I shake my head. "Nothing. Just trying to get open for the pass."

He narrows his eyes at me, but he lets it go.

I'm careful to avoid contact after that, but she's in my head now. I'm a little afraid of what having her in my head could mean for the upcoming season.

* * *

I'm not interested in going out Saturday night, but Travis, Jaxon, Austin, and Cory all head over to Coax. Instead of joining them, I call it an early night. I climb into the guest bed in Travis's place, and I call Tessa.

"Hey," she answers, and most people look distorted and goofy on video chat, but not my Tessa. She's as gorgeous as always.

"Anything exciting happen today?" I ask.

She chuckles. "Yes, actually. My mom threw me a surprise baby shower."

"I knew about it," I admit. "How was it?"

"You knew?" she asks, her tone accusatory.

"Who do you think gave her the key to our house?" I ask, and she giggles.

"Well, we're pretty much moved in now, and after the shower, the baby's all set. Everything we need is there. All that's missing is the two of us."

"I can't wait to be there. To move in with you. To wake up next to you," I say softly, keeping my voice low so I don't have to take shit from my teammates tomorrow should anyone happen to overhear me.

"I think we should get married," she blurts. Her eyes widen as she says the words.

"We are," I say with a yawn as the day's events catch up with me. "I proposed, remember?"

"Right, I know. What I mean is that we should do it soon. Before the baby gets here. Maybe…this week, even." Her tone is cautious as she throws out the idea.

"I thought you wanted to wait until after the baby so you'd fit into your dream dress." I sit up a little in bed. Is she serious?

"I do…" she trails off, and she starts over. "Well, I *did*, but the dress, the big wedding, the dream—none of it matters as much as being your wife matters, and I've been thinking a lot about everything. I think we should do it soon, and maybe in a year from now after the season ends and the Aces win the Super Bowl, we can have our big dream wedding."

"Where is this coming from?" I ask softly.

Her eyes look offended for a second, but she masks it quickly.

Before she can answer, I jump in. "It's not that I don't want to, Tess. Believe me, I do. I wouldn't have asked you if I wasn't ready to do it this very second. But why are you rushing it?"

She blows out a breath. "I want to be your wife. First and foremost, that's my answer. I've wanted to be your wife since I fell in love with you when I was twelve years old. I want that special connection that two people share where we commit to a lifetime together."

"But…?" I ask, trailing off.

"Well, there are other factors at play," she admits, and her eyes dart a little nervously around her bedroom before landing back on me. "You're a celebrity, and I'm terrified of the spotlight. I don't want our wedding all over the tabloids. I want it to be for us, and if we just do it before anybody can find out, it will be. And then there's the threat of our baby being taken away, even with Cam signing those papers…it's much better for my case if I can provide a stable home with two loving parents. And I want your dad there…" She trails off at the end.

I close my eyes as the reality of her words hits me.

I want my dad there, too. In fact, I want him to stand up with me as my best man. I want him to be proud of the man he raised.

I wish she was here so I could hold her in my arms. "Are you sure?" My brows draw together as I think it over. If I'm being honest, well, I've been ready to marry her what feels like my whole life.

"I'm positive. And I feel like the quicker we do it, the easier it'll be to keep it from becoming a media frenzy."

"So…city hall?" I ask.

"What do you think about a quickie Vegas wedding?" she asks.

I chuckle. "I think it's a fun idea, but is it safe for you to fly the closer we get to your due date?"

"I read that most airlines will let you fly all the way up to thirty-six weeks, so maybe if I'm cleared from all the risks at this week's appointment, I can make a quick trip out," she says.

"Why Vegas?" I ask softly. I can't pretend like I don't have reservations about coming back here for our wedding. There are too many people who could find out between now and then versus just heading to City Hall and taking care of it. There are far more complications in traveling.

"It seems important to you. And it's where our future is going to be, so it's important to me, too. Just pick a place that looks nice and book it for next week. If we have to cancel, we have to cancel."

My chest tightens that she wants to do this for me…for us. "Let's see what the doctor says this week, and if we get the green light, we can do it as soon as we can. If we don't get a green light on flying, I'll drive you myself."

"It's like twenty-four hours in the car, isn't it?" she asks with a giggle.

"Yeah," I admit. "Flying would definitely be more comfortable for the trip out, but we'll do what we have to in order to make this happen. Or we can do it in Iowa. I just want to be married to you. Forever."

"That's all I want, too. I love you, Tristan." Her voice trembles with emotion, and I feel it, too.

"T and T, baby. I love you, too," I murmur.

We end the call, and I start looking up places where we can do this. Almost every major hotel has a chapel, but nearly all of them are booked solid. We could do one of the drive-thru ones off-Strip, but she said to pick somewhere nice. It might be a quickie Vegas wedding with just our parents in attendance, but that doesn't mean it has to be cheesy or gaudy.

It just has to be perfect for *us*.

I find an opening at a small chapel inside the Venetian for next Friday night, and I book it. It'll give us three days after her doctor appointment to get to Vegas if we need to drive. I book a suite at the hotel, too, for Thursday through Monday, along with rooms for my parents and her mom.

I'll call the hotel tomorrow to arrange appointments for our wedding attire and all the other things she'll want for our special day, and then I stare up at my ceiling.

I just got out of a marriage, and I've barely had time to just be single—to just be *me*.

But I know who I am. I was lost a long time…seven years, to be exact, but I found myself the moment our eyes connected across our bedroom windows at the end of January.

I can't wait to get started on our future together.

Just as I'm about to drift off to sleep with a smile lifting my lips, my phone notifies me of a new text.

Unknown: *Your friends are at the club. Where are you?*

My chest races.

Who the hell is this?

I blocked the unknown number last time. Is this somebody else?

It's time to find out. I'm done ignoring, done blocking…done playing games.

Me: *Who is this?*

Unknown: *Didn't block me this time?*

Who has the time to get a new number simply to harass somebody else?

Savannah.

It *has* to be her.

Me: *I'm done playing games. What do you want?*

Unknown: *Don't you play games for a living?*

I blow out a breath, and before I can respond, another text comes through.

No MISTAKE

Unknown: *You'll find out soon enough. [wink emoji]*

It has to be empty threats.

I block the number and toss my phone aside as I try to get some rest.

But the smile lifting my lips is gone, and peaceful slumber escapes me.

CHAPTER 14

Tessa

I kiss his face like he's been gone for a year, and he laughs as he clutches me in his arms. We're standing in the foyer of our new home, and he just walked in the door about four seconds ago.

"Am I going to be punished, sir?" I ask.

He chuckles as his eyes meet mine. "Do you want to be?"

I squirm a little. "Yes and no. I mean, I'd like to have some fun, too, if you know what I mean."

"Let's hope you're cleared tomorrow at the doctor. And speaking of that, I booked us a chapel at the Venetian for Friday. Does that sound good?" he asks.

"We're getting married on Friday?" My tone is filled with awe and I'm sure my eyes are dreamy and faraway.

I never thought this moment would come.

He nods. "Should we tell our parents?"

"Let's have them over for dinner tonight and surprise them," I suggest.

He nods, and then excitement overtakes me. I kiss him once more before I grab his hand and rush around the house, dragging him into room after room as I show him every last detail and all the work I've put in over the last few days along with all the gifts from the baby shower.

The house kept me occupied and quieted my mind from worrying about Stephanie, about Tristan being out of town…about everything.

I take him into the baby's room last, and I show off the new purple and gray nursery filled with little forest friends. I found a wall decal featuring a tree with lavender and white leaves, and bunnies, foxes, and squirrels run around in the scene beneath it.

It's perfect. It's cute while also promoting a sense of adventurous wonder—exactly what I'd want for my sweet little girl.

"This is incredible, Tess," he murmurs as he looks around the room. He walks over and touches the decal. "I love this."

I smile proudly upon it. "So do I."

He walks over and circles his arms around me, burying his face in my neck. "You're already such a great mother to our baby and she's not even here yet. How did I get so lucky?"

Tears fill my eyes. We made it through the run of bad luck. It's our turn for something good now, and I hope and pray we're through the worst of it and on the other side.

He presses a soft kiss to my collarbone, and I squeeze him. "I'm the lucky one," I say softly. I don't need to voice aloud how alone I felt on the drive from Chicago to Fallon Ridge when I first moved back. I was leaving a job I loved, pregnant and alone, to come live with my mother who I'd barely spoken to in the last seven years.

Now my mom and I are closer than ever, my baby has a father, I'll soon have a husband who happens to be the man of every dream I've had since I was twelve, and we own the house on the corner.

It feels like life couldn't get any more perfect than it is.

And then the doorbell rings.

No MISTAKE

You know in movies how the doorbell rings and it's that low-toned sound of doom and gloom?

That's sort of how it sounds in my mind.

Tristan kisses me once more before running down the stairs to see who it is, and the thought of doom and gloom rings true as Tristan throws the door open to find my half-sister behind it.

I just saw her yesterday at the shower.

Why is she back today?

"Stephanie," he says quietly. "What are you doing here?"

"Oh, you're back from Vegas?" she asks flatly.

"I'm back," he verifies, and I walk a little more slowly down the steps behind him. "Now's not a good time." He offers no other information or excuses, and I wish I could talk to her like that.

"Why not?" she challenges.

"I'm sorry, but it's personal," he says. "Thank you for understanding."

He moves to shut the door, but she's quick with putting her foot in the doorway so he can't close it.

"Wait," she says, and Tristan turns to give me a look that says *what the fuck is up with her* without actually voicing the words.

"What?" he asks, and he sounds exasperated as he turns back to face her.

"I just want to talk to my sister," she says.

"*Half*-sister," he corrects, and she rolls her eyes.

"I, uh, didn't get a chance to chat with her much yesterday, and I just wanted to say what a nice shower it was."

It feels like something that could've been handled with a phone call, but she probably thinks I wouldn't have picked up if I saw it was her calling.

And she's probably right to think that.

"What's up, Stephanie?" I ask, and my voice sounds tired…mainly because I *am* tired of dealing with her.

"Did you find a scrunchie at your mom's house? It's my favorite and I think I dropped it somewhere," she says.

"You drove all the way from Kewanee to find a scrunchie?" Tristan asks.

I hold back a giggle. "It's her favorite, Tristan," I say, coming up to the side of him and lightly knocking my knuckles against his chest. I look at her. "I haven't seen one, but you're welcome to mine." I pull a hair tie off my wrist and get an idea. "See if it fits," I suggest, and she takes it and slides it onto her wrist.

"Maybe later. Well, I guess I'll see you around," she says.

The second her foot is out of the doorway, Tristan slams the door.

"See you around?" he murmurs to me, lacing his arms around my waist. "She lives forty-five minutes away. It's weird how she keeps showing up," he says.

"Do you think we should add it to the police report?" I ask.

"It couldn't hurt." He lets go of me and pulls his phone out of his pocket. He sends off a text.

"What was that?" I ask.

"I told Walt we have some new information to share with him." He glances at his phone. "He said he's driving around, and he'll be right over."

Walt shows up as promised two minutes later, and we invite him in.

"Any new details on the case?" Tristan asks, and we take a seat on the new furniture in the front room.

Walt shakes his head. "We haven't figured out who it is, but what I can tell you is that unless there's some other crime happening, there's not much we can do. Online impersonation happens all the time, and while it's terrible you're being targeted, there's not really anything illegal about it."

"Even if she's making money off it?" Tristan asks.

He shrugs. "If she's doing anything to make Tessa liable in court or something that might cause her to pay money, then we could pursue false impersonation. But there's little else to go on."

"What if the person I think is doing it is also stalking me?" I ask.

Tristan's brows dip. "You think she's stalking you?"

I shrug. "She shows up all the time uninvited. She knows things about me…and her Instagram…"

"Stalking is a crime when you feel threatened by her," Walt says. "Who is it?"

"It's my half-sister," I say. "I just met her when my father died, and I think she has become obsessed with me."

"Obsessed how?" Walt asks.

"She's mentioned a few times to me how I have everything, and she seems to think she has nothing." I shrug as I start to question whether I'm going a little crazy—whether I'm being too hard on her. "She seems harmless enough, but I don't really know her. She's just very interested in everything I do."

He nods. "Give me her name and I can look into her as a person of interest."

"Stephanie Taylor. She lives in Kewanee, Illinois."

"The tattoo," Tristan says.

"Oh," I say. "Right. We saw the edge of a tattoo in one of the videos, but I don't know if Stephanie has one or not."

"I'll see what I can do," Walt says. He flips open a notepad and jots some things down, and then he sticks it in his pocket and stands. "You two have a great day."

"Thanks, Walt," I say as we walk him to the door.

I feel better having him on our side, like he'll figure out a solution here so this weirdness with Stephanie will stop.

I don't know how else to get her out of my life, and the more I interact with her, the more certain I am that I need to figure it out.

CHAPTER 15

Tristan

"Let's see," the doctor says, taking a look at the ultrasound images. "Everything is looking good. You've been on pelvic rest for almost four weeks now, and that's usually the recommended time. I'm going to go ahead and clear you today. I'm not seeing any real risks and your placenta has moved up."

I exchange a glance with Tessa.

"Does this mean I can fly?" she asks.

The doctor nods. "I don't see why not. I wouldn't consider you at-risk, so you're safe to fly up to thirty-six weeks. You can always call the office if you have concerns. Take a copy of your health record with you, and I can provide proof of your due date just in case the airline needs it." She glances at me then back at Tessa. "Where are you planning to go?"

"We're hopping a plane to Vegas to get married," Tessa says proudly, her eyes on me as she squeezes my hand.

I grin, and I pull her hand to my lips.

"Congratulations," the doctor says, a smile on her lips, too. "Enjoy your trip." She winks at Tessa. "And the honeymoon."

"So sex is okay?" Tessa asks, and her cheeks redden with mortification that she just asked that question.

The doctor smiles. "Totally okay. In fact, sometimes it can help get labor moving. You're safe to resume normal activity."

Tessa asks a few more questions, and then the doctor leaves.

I raise a brow. "No more pelvic rest, huh?"

A smile tips her lips. "Ever think of getting nasty in an obstetrician's office?"

"Only in my wildest fantasies," I murmur. She's still wearing the paper gown the doctor handed over. "I mean, you're already naked."

She laughs. "True, but I don't have doctor office fantasies. I do, however, have fantasies about every room in our new house."

"Then get your sweet ass in the car so we can start christening all of them," I growl.

She doesn't hesitate.

The twenty-five minute drive home feels endless, but my tires squeal as I pull into the driveway. I cut the engine and jump out of the car, and Tessa's giggling at me as she climbs calmly out of the passenger seat.

"What?" I ask.

"You just seem like you're in a rush," she says as she moves around the car toward the front porch, where my key is already being shoved into the door to unlock it.

"I am." I pause what I'm doing and I turn toward her. I lower my lips toward her neck and press a kiss there, and then I murmur softly into her ear. "It's been almost four weeks since I've been inside you, and I can't wait another second."

Her cheeks flush. "I can't, either. But I'm still a little nervous."

I turn back toward the door and open it, holding my hand out for her to go first. "The doctor cleared you, babe. She said you're safe to resume activity, remember?"

No MISTAKE

She nods and squirms a little as she steps to move past me and into the house. She pauses in front of me, her body close and her lips touching mine softly. "Let's do it."

That's all I need to hear. I move through the door and kick it shut behind me, and I haul her into my arms. My lips crash down to hers, and she squeals at the sudden movement. "Where first?" I ask.

"Don't care," she mumbles between kisses, her mouth never leaving mine.

I break from her long enough to kneel down and slide her panties down her legs. She's wearing a dress today, perfect for what I have planned, and I reach under her dress and slide my fingers up her thighs and right into her folds.

She's slick with wet heat, and I plunge a finger in.

"Oh God," she says, grabbing onto the top of my head to steady herself.

I lift her dress and stick my head under it. It's dark under here, but I need to taste her.

She widens her stance as I spread her pussy with my fingers and slide my tongue through her.

"Oh fuck," I hum against her. "You taste so fucking good."

She jolts when I touch my tongue to her clit, and I suck on it as I thrust my finger back in.

I drive my finger in and out as I duck out from under the dress, and her head is tipped back in pleasure as I finger her.

I remove my hand from her body and move to a stand, where I unbuckle my belt, lower my zipper, and pull out my cock.

I stroke it a few times, the tip glistening with my arousal, and then I let go, taking both her hands in mine. I sit on the couch in the front room then guide her down so she sets her legs on either side of me. I grasp my cock again as she positions herself over me. I slide in, and we both grunt at the feel of being connected in this way again.

"Fuck, I've been waiting weeks for this. It's even better than I remember," I say softly. She's slick with need for me, for this, and I move my hands to her ass and help guide her up and down so her legs don't have to do all the work.

"You feel so good, too," she says, her words a little tentative like she isn't used to talking during sex. "You make me so wet." She closes her eyes and tips her head back, enjoying the moment.

I'm surprised when the words slip out of my mouth. "Look at me."

Her eyes fly open and connect with mine. Hers are hazy with desire, and it's a real turn-on to see how hot she is for me.

"Good girl," I murmur, and her face contorts with pleasure, like I just gave her a tiny orgasm with my words of praise.

I go for more, voicing all the words I'm thinking. "Your body is so fucking incredible, Tessa."

"Keep doing what you're doing," she cries on moan.

I allow one of my pinky fingers to inch over toward her ass, and she squirms a little on top of me as a bit of uncertainty moves through her eyes. The shift in her movement causes my balls to seize, and I want to slow this down. I *have* to slow this down. I want it to last forever, but if that's not an option, just a little longer.

I inch my finger over a little more, and I graze against the hole there. She closes her eyes as she groans, and I can tell she likes it.

"Eyes on me," I say.

Her eyes fly open again, and there's a need in them that was absent before. I push my pinky in, and her mouth forms an *O* as I pull it out. A high-pitched squeak comes out of her, and then she really starts to move, riding me harder as I move my pinky in and out of her.

"Someday I'll fuck you there," I murmur, and my words are enough to send her flying over the edge.

"Oh God, Tristan, I'm coming, I'm coming," she cries out, and she fights to keep her eyes on mine as she comes. I watch her face as it twists in the sweet agony of release, and I feel her body tighten over my cock as she hits her climax, the contractions doing something incredible to me that sends me into my own release.

I pump up into her, a loud roar filling the room as I allow my finger to slip out of her so I can hold on tightly. I keep my eyes on hers the whole time so she can see me through my release, too, and it's a beautifully intimate moment I've never experienced before.

When it's all over, she lifts off me and settles onto the couch beside me, her panties still on the floor.

"Well, that's one room christened," she says.

I chuckle. "One new piece of furniture broken in." I wrench my arm behind her so I can pull her in closer to me. "God, I missed that. I missed *you*."

"I missed you, too," she says, and she tips her head back to press a kiss to my jaw.

"What did you think of the pinky?" I ask.

She shifts so she's not looking at me as she answers. "I liked it."

"It's okay to look at me when you say it," I say softly. "There's nothing to be embarrassed about."

"I've never done that before, but it was...really freaking hot."

I chuckle. "The way your eyes heated over when I did it confirmed that, but I never want to do anything your uncomfortable with."

She shakes her head. "I wasn't uncomfortable. And I might be interested in trying that again."

"Your wish is my command. Can I get you anything?" I ask.

"Well, you did just fill me with nearly four weeks' worth of your build-up, except for that one punishment plus whatever handies you've given yourself, so I'd like to use the restroom before I ruin our new couch."

I can't help my laugh. I tuck my dick back into my boxers then stand. I reach out a hand to pull her up, and she accepts my help before practically running to the bathroom.

A smile tips my lips as a wave of love rushes through me.

I love our life together. I love *her*.

I laugh out loud even though I'm alone in the room.

I've never had a woman dart out of the room after sex because she was afraid she was going to ruin furniture with all the come I left inside her, but that's one of the things I love about Tessa Taylor. She's herself, and she's one hundred percent real with me all the time.

And *that* is what the foundation of our future is being built upon.

A wave of guilt hits me.

I've told her I don't need to know more about the seven years we spent apart, and a big reason why is so that I could hide my own secrets. The thing with Tiffany, the third floor of the club and the aftercare thing…these are things Tessa is better off not knowing. They're things in my history I'm ashamed of, and they don't matter now, anyway…much like the things she did in our time apart don't matter to me.

But if we're building a foundation of trust before we get married in a few days' time, she deserves the truth.

All of it.

CHAPTER 16

Tristan

I sling my duffel bag over my shoulder. It's the last of my belongings still at my parents' house, and as ready as I am to move in with Tessa, to wake up beside her every morning, to hold her in my arms every night, to brush my teeth next to her as we establish our morning routine…I'm still a little hesitant to leave my mom and dad's house.

It's not the fear of growing up or anything like that. I've already moved out, and I hadn't been back to this place in a long, long time.

It's more than that.

It's the fear of missing out on time with my dad.

And on that note, I head out to the garage before I take the walk down the block to my new house, where my truck is already parked.

My mom is still at the salon, but my dad is in the garage sanding down a project, and when he turns off the sander, he glances up at me. "You all packed?" he asks.

I nod and set my bag down on the treadmill. I sit on the edge of it. "How are you feeling?" I ask.

"What was the only request I had of you when I first told you I was sick?" he asks.

I glance up at him. "Don't treat you like you're dying."

He holds up his hands as if to say *yep, that's it.* "I'm fine. But stop. I'll tell you when I'm not fine. I know you don't want to leave because you're worried about me, but you can't let what's happening to *me* stop you from doing everything you want to do in your life. Do you hear me?"

"Yeah, I hear you," I say.

"Now get outta here." He jerks his thumb toward the door.

I laugh. "Come over for dinner tonight. You and Mom. Tess and I have something to tell you."

He raises his brows. "Do I get a preview?"

I hold up my hands. "All I'm saying is clear your schedule for the weekend because you're coming to Vegas. But it's all very hush-hush and Tessa wants to tell you two and her mom together."

He chuckles. "All right. But is this what you want, son?"

"Yeah," I say softly. "It's all I ever wanted."

He walks over and sets a hand on my shoulder. "You walked down the wrong road a while with that ex-wife of yours."

I press my lips together and set a hand over his. "Somebody I really admire always told me to fix my mistakes. I'm a work in progress, but I've got one checked off the list."

"Love you, kiddo," he says, and he squeezes my shoulder.

"Love you, too, Pops," I say. I give him a hug before I sling my bag over my shoulder and head out the door toward home.

Tessa's car is beside my truck in the driveway, and I can't help but admire how they look beside each other as I leap up the steps and onto the porch. I ring the bell, and she opens it a second later with a giggle.

"It's your home, too," she says. "You could just walk in, you know."

A smile tips my lips. "Come out here."

She does, and I sweep her up into my arms. "Oh my God, Tristan! You're going to hurt yourself lifting me like that!"

"Stop," I say, and I press my lips to hers to quiet her. "It's tradition to carry the woman over the threshold, isn't it?"

"I think that's when you're married."

"Well, for us, it'll be any time I damn well feel like it." I walk through the front door with her in my arms, both of us laughing the entire time.

That's all I've ever wanted. A lifetime of laughter, of peace and harmony. Of love.

The last time I felt those things was the last time I was with her. The women in between never even came close—most especially my ex-wife.

I got it right this time.

I feel it in my blood.

"How was saying goodbye to your mom?" I ask as I set her down. I toss my duffel by the stairs and follow her into the kitchen, where she resumes her task of putting dishes into a cabinet.

"You know, it was harder than I thought it would be," she admits.

"Same." I press my lips together. "It's going to be so weird to be in Fallon Ridge and *not* sleep at my parents' house."

"Or talk to each other through our windows," she says.

I hadn't thought of that. As many benefits as there will be to us living together, there are a lot of things about our old houses I'll miss.

"If you ever want to chat through the window, I'm sure our parents would love for us to come visit," I say, wrapping my arms around her waist from behind as she stretches to get some bowls on a higher shelf. I set my hands over her swollen stomach, a ripple of love for both her and the baby coursing down my spine. "But this is where it begins, babe. It's where we start our life together. Not the life our parents wanted for us as they raised us in those houses on Oak Tree Lane, but the life we want for ourselves right here on Main Street."

She spins in my arms. "I love you," she says, and she presses her lips to mine.

"I love you, too," I say, and I allow my hands to wander down to her ass.

She bats my hand away, and I chuckle. "None of that yet, sir. We have a house to clean for our first dinner party. I'm going to sweep, and I need you to finish cleaning out the dishwasher."

"But I don't know where anything goes," I protest.

She laughs. "You'll figure it out."

The doorbell rings, and my brows dip as I glance at Tessa. Then I walk over to answer it.

"Walt," I say in greeting when I see him standing on our porch. I wave him in.

Tessa walks in the room behind us. "Any news for us?"

"Good afternoon," he begins, as if that'll soften the blow of his next words. He sighs. "Turns out we can't do much about the online impersonation. What she's doing is immoral, but unless it's true identity theft, it's not really illegal. I can confirm we saw a tattoo on the neck. It appears to be angel wings with some sort of date written in. It's hard to make out from the video, but it looks like possibly May twenty-something."

"Seventh?" Tessa asks.

"We think it's probably either a one or a seven."

"My dad's birthday was May twenty-seventh," she says, glancing at me.

"Stephanie?" I ask.

She nods. "It has to be."

No MISTAKE

Walt jumps in. "Do you think this woman might be dangerous?"

My eyes meet Tessa's, and she shrugs.

"I don't know," she says to Walt. "I don't know her very well, but she seems harmless enough."

"Then track what she's doing, when or where she shows up," he says. "Keep a record for us, and if you have any concerns, now that we have an open case, bring them to us. We might be able to make a move on the stalking charges, but only if you feel unsafe. If she doesn't pose a threat, then she's just an annoyance that won't go away."

"That's it?" I ask. "All you can do is tell Tessa to keep a record of when she shows up?"

"I'm sorry." He shrugs. "I wish I had better news for you, but that's really all we can do at this point."

"Thanks for the update," I say, and he nods at us both on his way out. I glance at Tessa once the door shuts behind her. "You okay?"

She nods. "Yes, I'm okay. It's disappointing that she can just do that and get away with it, but maybe I should just confront her and ask her to stop. Or find out why she's doing it."

"The more I hear about her, the more convinced I become that she wants to *be* you. Look at all you've got, babe. You had a successful career as a nurse, you moved back home, you're having a baby, you're getting married. You had the father she wanted. She looks at you and thinks you have everything," I say gently. "And she's a little unhinged."

"That's not helping," she says, placing her hand on her stomach. "That's only making it more alarming."

"I know," I concede. "But we're moving to Vegas, and we'll be further away from her. It'll be okay."

She nods. "That does make me feel a little better."

I'm not entirely convinced it does, though…and I don't feel much better myself.

The house is immaculate when our parents arrive at six-thirty. Soft music plays in the background, candles are lit, and Tessa has even put out little cheese and cracker plates as appetizers before our food from the Pizza Joint arrives. We take them on the grand tour, and they're in love with what we've done with the place.

"It was all Tessa," I say, giving credit where credit is due. She preens under my words, and she blushes at our parents' compliments.

"We have some news," Tessa says, her eyes edging over to me. I give her a quick nod, and she clears her throat. "We're getting married."

Her mom's brows dip as she glances at my parents, who also look confused by the announcement. "We know, honey," she says. "You told us."

"This Friday in Vegas," I finish, just as we had planned. "And we want the three of you to be there. I've already booked rooms and flights for everyone."

Tessa's mom's eyes go wide as she slaps a hand over her mouth. My mom squeals, and my dad looks wholly unsurprised.

My mom smacks his arm. "Did you already know?"

He chuckles. "I suspected."

"Are you okay to travel?" my mom asks Tessa, and she nods.

"The doctor cleared me of any risks at my appointment today," she says.

Hugs are issued all around, and it's a night for celebrating. My dad and I drink whiskey, and my mom and Janet toast with wine, and we gorge ourselves on the best pizza and pasta in town.

No **MISTAKE**

Our parents leave after they help clean, and then it's just the two of us in the house we own as we start our life together.

I turn off the lights in the kitchen so the flicker of the candles bounces off the walls, and I turn up the music as a The Calling's "Wherever You Will Go" pipes into the kitchen. I take my future wife in my arms.

She giggles a little at first as I swing her around in the candlelight, and then her eyes meet mine. We dance as we both think toward the future with hope and excitement over how many more dances there will be in this very place.

When the song is over, we dance to another one, and then we blow out the candles, and she leads me up the stairs to our bedroom.

Before we fall asleep in our new bed in our new home, we make love as we use our bodies to strengthen our bond and show each other how deep our feelings run.

And as I drift off to sleep, I push away the feeling that nothing this good will last forever. Instead of focusing on the fear of it all falling apart, I decide to revel in its joy for however long we have it.

CHAPTER 17

Tessa

I draw in a deep breath as I click the call button, determined to get to the bottom of this Stephanie business.

"Hey Tessa!" Stephanie answers, and she's overly enthusiastic.

Avoid her.

Make notes of when you see her.

Stay away from her.

I ignore all the sage advice from the people who most care about me in the entire world, and instead I follow my gut.

"I was thinking of coming to Kewanee to see you. I thought maybe you could show me your downtown area so I can get a feel for what you're doing with the craft fair. Are you busy?" I ask. I figure we can do this on her home turf, make her comfortable, and then ask the hard-hitting questions.

I have to.

I need this resolved before I go to Vegas to marry Tristan. I need to have answers before I have this baby.

And something struck me this morning when I woke up.

I've largely ignored her and written her off. I've blamed her for this JustFans thing without ever *asking* her.

What if I just ask her?

Tristan thinks it's a terrible idea, but he said he'd come with me. My guess is he's doing it in some effort to keep me safe, but as weird as Stephanie can be, I really don't think she poses an actual threat.

But I also don't know her that well because I haven't allowed myself the chance to.

Maybe there's a perfectly reasonable explanation for all the weirdness where she's concerned, or maybe I'll leave, get on a plane to Vegas, block her number, and never look back.

We're short on time since we leave for Vegas tonight, but I convinced him to take a detour through Kewanee on the way to the airport.

"That would be amazing!" she squeals. "When are you thinking?"

"I'm heading out of town tonight, so I was thinking I could swing by on my way to the airport. Say in the next hour or so?" I ask.

"Perfect! I'm home, so I'll just text over my address and you can meet me here. Sound okay?"

"Yep," I say, and I nod at Tristan, who sighs, but then like the amazing future husband he's going to be, he grabs our suitcases and loads them into his truck.

An hour later, we're pulling into the driveway of a small house that looks like it could use a fresh coat of paint. The front yard is covered in weeds, and a weather-beaten old rocking chair sits on the front stoop. It looks like it would fall apart if someone actually sat on it.

"This is it," I say.

"Are you sure about this?" Tristan asks.

I nod. "Let's just settle this once and for all."

He walks up behind me as I ring the bell, and when Stephanie opens the door, she looks excited to see me here.

And then her face falls as she spots Tristan standing behind me.

"Come on in," she says, and we enter right into a family room with a couch pointed at a television. It's a small space, big enough for the couch and a small coffee table, and she motions toward the couch to tell us to sit. It's neat and tidy in here, like she ran around cleaning and vacuuming the second she knew a guest was coming. "Can I get you anything?"

I shake my head. "We can't stay too long."

"Okay. I'll be right back. Make yourselves at home," she says.

She disappears for a moment, and when she returns, she's carrying a chair that looks like it came from her kitchen table. She sets it in the small entryway by the front door and sits.

"So good to see you both," she says, her eyes edging nervously to Tristan. "Did you want to go downtown to see where the fair is going to be set up?"

"I uh...I actually didn't come to talk about the fair," I say, and Tristan sits quietly beside me, though he seems to stiffen at my words. My eyes are down on my hands.

"You didn't?" Stephanie asks, and she sounds confused.

I shake my head as I glance up at her. "I need to ask you something."

Her brows dip. "Okay..."

"Are you impersonating me online?" I blurt.

Her brows dip as her hand moves to her chest in horror. "What?" she gasps.

"Someone has been dancing naked for money and pretending to be me on the site JustFans. Is that you?" I ask.

"JustFans...I would never! How can you even ask me that?" she asks, and she truly does sound offended.

I glance at Tristan, and he nods.

"It's just…I saw your photos on Instagram. I saw you had gone places I had gone with our dad and took the same sorts of photos. It just seemed a little—um…*strange* to me. Like you were already impersonating me in that way, so maybe this JustFans thing is you, too," I say, stumbling over my words.

Her cheeks flush. "I can't believe you'd come in my own home and accuse me of such a horrible thing!"

"But the Instagram pictures…" I say, trying to get an answer for that out of her if she's not going to admit to the naked dancing.

"Tessa, I was never *impersonating* you. I wanted to know what it felt like to have your childhood. I wanted to feel his presence in those places since I never got to do those things with him when he was here. It was my way of mourning so much of the loss I've had in the last year. He did those things with *you*, and he never did them with *me*. But to impersonate you online? I'm hurt you think so little of me."

"I don't think little of you," I say softly. "I don't even *know* you."

"Because you haven't *tried* to get to know me," she says flatly. "I lost my father seven months ago, effectively erasing any chance at all of having any sort of relationship with him. The only way I even have a shot at getting to know who he was is through you."

I stare at her as her words plow into me. "How'd he keep you quiet?" I ask softly.

Her brows dip. "What?"

"Why didn't you come introduce yourself before he died? Why did you wait until after?"

She sighs, and then she glances around her house and holds her hands up to indicate the entire thing. "He bought my mom this house. He paid for my college classes. He tried to take care of us monetarily, and he threatened to take it all away if I told anyone the truth." She shakes her head. "I lost my mother two months before he passed. I was scared of getting cut off financially. Scared I wouldn't be able to stay in this house. Scared I wouldn't be able to put food on the table. I wanted to reach out to you so many times, but I couldn't."

I just sit quietly, shock running through me her words start to register.

"She was my best friend, but she was also very sick, and I was her caretaker for the last three years. I lost all my friends when they moved away after college, and I was stuck here caring for her. I'm all alone, living in my mother's house in a tiny town I can't seem to break out of, but at least I had my father sending me money and doing what he could to take care of me even though he couldn't physically be here…until I didn't. And when I finally met you, I was so excited to finally have the sister I always wanted. But you just constantly push me away, or brush me off, or have a reason why you don't want anything to do with me."

"Oh, Stephanie. I'm so, so sorry," I say softly. I stand and move over toward her, and I hold out a hand. She takes it and stands, too, as a new understanding dawns on me.

She has literally nobody.

She found me and immediately clung onto me before she took any chance of getting to know me, and rather than accept her and take her in as my half-sister, I resisted the clinginess and kept pushing her away.

"I can't even begin to imagine what you've been through." I pull her into a hug, and I turn us so her back is toward Tristan. I meet his eyes with mine, and I gently sweep her hair to the side just to be totally certain.

He shakes his head a little.

No tattoo.

I hug her a little closer as regret tightens my chest. "I'm so sorry I haven't been accepting. You have to understand that with my relationship with Tristan, a lot of people try to take advantage of him, which in turn means of me, too. I haven't allowed myself to be open to the possibility of a relationship with you for lots of reasons—reasons maybe we can talk about someday, but not now. I'd love it if we could start over, though. Maybe get to know one another. Become friends. Become sisters, even—because I always wanted a sister, too."

She pulls back. "You mean it?"

"I'd love to try. But I also think we need to set some boundaries, okay?"

She glances at Tristan then back at me, and she nods. "Okay."

"No more unexpected, surprise drop-ins," I say, ticking off the things that bother me most.

She nods.

"No more fighting with Tristan. I'm marrying him, and we're a package deal."

She shoots him a glare, but she reluctantly nods a little. "Fine. But he has to be nice to me, too."

I look at him and raise my brows, and he holds up both hands innocently. "Promise."

"And most important of all, Stephanie...just be *you*," I say. "Stop trying to be me."

"I wasn't—" She starts to protest, but I cut her off.

"You started a town craft fair because I did. You said you were going to go back to school for nursing. You cut your hair like mine. Just stop. Please. Be you, because *that* is who I want to get to know."

"Fine," she mumbles. "But can I just tell you one thing?"

My brows knit together as I narrow my eyes at her. "What?"

"I'm interviewing for a new position."

No **MISTAKE**

"Where?" I ask.

She clears her throat. "Lakeshore Pediatrics."

I can't help a small laugh. She doesn't have her RN, and I'm guessing she's applying for a tech job. And I think it would be a great fit for her…as long as she can be herself.

"I'll put in a good word for you." I wink at her, and she laughs.

We spend a little more time chatting, and she tells me she's going to cancel the craft fair. I feel a little sense of relief at that, and I already see her starting to come out of her shell a little. I feel like I'm already starting to get to know *Stephanie*, not Tessa two-point-oh.

We have to leave to catch our flight, so we say our goodbyes with promises to do lunch soon. And we will. I really have always wanted a sister, and even though she came about in a strange way, I do think we could eventually become friends if I give her the chance and she sticks to the boundaries we set.

But one question remains, and I ask it in the car once we hit the highway.

"So if it's not her doing the JustFans thing…who is it?"

CHAPTER 18

Tessa

The plane touches down, and my eyes are out the window while my hand is planted firmly in Tristan's. I spot the hotels I've only ever seen in pictures as I stare out the window, and it's every bit as magical as I thought it might be.

"How far do you live from all that?" I ask.

He shrugs. "I *lived* about fifteen minutes away in a kickass house, but the only way I could get Savannah to leave was to move out."

"Where would you want to live?" I ask.

"If I was buying, I'd probably want to go somewhere around Luke's neighborhood. It's close to the Complex and it's in a good school district." He reaches over and lays his hand on my stomach, and it hits me that I'm *moving* here.

We're going to be raising a child here.

It looks incredible from the window, but I truly have no idea what to expect. Vegas always seemed like the city of sin and bright lights, but now I'll call it home.

My father must be rolling over in his grave.

What a strange time to think of him.

"Do you like it here?" I ask. If anyone would give me an honest answer, it's Tristan.

"I love it," he says. "The mountains, the palm trees, the weather…it's like being on vacation all the time when you're used to icy cold winters and humidity and snow."

"Even after three years here?" I ask.

He nods as he averts his eyes to the window.

I squeeze his hand in mine as I keep my eyes on him rather than the scenery. "So is this where you want to settle?"

He lifts a shoulder. "It's hard to say. It's easier to have a home base away from all this because none of it's stable. I could be traded, or hurt, or not renewed if I have a shitty season. There are a lot of factors."

"Is that why you bought the house on the corner?"

He leans in and presses a soft kiss beneath my ear. "No. That was for you."

My chest tightens and my eyes fill with tears. How did I ever get so lucky as to find this man not just once, but twice in one lifetime?

Since Tristan sprung for first class tickets, we're the first people to walk off the plane. We're ushered to some private terminal where our bags from baggage claim are delivered to us, and then we get into a car to take us to our hotel.

I've never actually experienced the celebrity lifestyle before, but I suppose I could find a way to get used to all this. It's quite different from how I'm accustomed to traveling.

Get on the plane when you're called. Fight for your seat and hope and pray you don't get stuck in a middle. Wait at baggage claim, sweating like a pig with everybody else, and then fight your way to the front when you see your bag. Wait for a cab, trying to calm down after the fight at baggage claim and the rush to get in line so you're not waiting forever for your ride.

I like this version better. Maybe I'm scared of the spotlight, but this could be a decent trade-off for it.

No **MISTAKE**

I'm in awe as I look out the window. We're a street away from the Strip, but when the driver turns onto it, even in the daytime without the lights flashing against the dark night sky…it's simply magical.

We turn into one of the gorgeous hotels, and the driver drops us by the door. We walk through the lobby toward the reception area and I'm simply in awe of everything around me.

It's like I've been transported to Italy as I walk the indoor area outfitted with huge chandeliers and beautiful works of art. After we check in, our bags are taken up to our room for us.

"Want to go up or want to look around?" Tristan asks me.

I opt for looking around, so we head outside to watch the gondolas as they move romantically along, and we watch the people as they hustle and bustle their way down the Strip. We walk a few doors down and have lunch on the patio of a restaurant, people-watching and enjoying our time as a couple visiting Las Vegas.

"It's rare I get to see the Strip from this angle," Tristan says. "I usually only come down here for team events or club appearances."

"Do you go to a lot of those?" I take a sip of my Sprite.

"Clubs?" he clarifies, and when I nod, he shrugs. "Not a *lot*." He shifts a little and averts his gaze back to the people passing by, caught up in their own lives and totally oblivious to the fact that a huge football superstar is sitting at this table watching them. "Paid appearances are usually not very exciting, as I've mentioned before. Every move is dissected thanks to social media. I've been to some—uh…*private* clubs that tend to be lower pressure."

"*Private* clubs?" I repeat. "Like for rich people?"

He chuckles, and I get the sense he's a little uncomfortable. "Sort of, I guess." He pauses, and he opens his mouth to say something else when the server comes by to ask if we need anything else.

"Just the check," I say. I'm ready to explore some more, ready to check out the chapel where we're getting married in two days' time, ready to go to our room for a sex break or maybe even a nap. A snap? I read about that on one of the mom blogs—it's sex followed by a nap, apparently one of the few ways to actually fit in nookie once you have kids.

I'm torn between wanting to relax and wanting to immerse myself in the full Vegas experience.

We're walking back toward our hotel when a woman does a double take at Tristan. Her eyes slide over to me then down to my pregnant stomach, and I feel suddenly self-conscious.

Does she recognize him? Is she instantly judging me and deciding I'm not good enough for someone like him? Will we end up on social media?

Will it always be like this?

I'm sure Cam's wife hasn't forgotten about her threats to me even though he signed the paperwork giving me full custody. If I'm plastered all over social media, it'll just be a reminder to her. I'm not sure what she wants out of all this, but I can't be linked publicly to Cam. It won't just affect Paul anymore. Now Tristan is involved. His reputation will be on the line, too, plus his family, and Cam's kids, and it's all too much.

Fear seeps into me and swims in my blood. I am meant to be with Tristan. He knows it and I know it, and that's all that matters. But these forces continue to try to tear us apart, and I'm suddenly terrified we're rushing into this marriage thing with all the wrong intentions.

Another woman gives me the eye like I'm not good enough for the man clutching my hand.

Maybe it's all in my overactive imagination.

No MISTAKE

Maybe it's the pregnancy hormones.

Maybe it's pre-wedding jitters.

Or maybe it's none of those things, and I have legitimate reasons to be nervous about all this.

"Tess?" Tristan asks, and his voice sounds far away as he snaps me out of my thoughts. "Are you okay?"

"I'm okay," I whisper.

"You're squeezing my hand so tightly and your face is pale. Do you want to sit for a second?" he asks.

"I'm okay," I repeat, a little louder this time. I draw in a shaky breath.

"Tristan?" some woman says, and when I glance up at her, I find a gorgeous woman getting closer to him. She wears a gold string bikini and a huge headdress with fruit and feathers. It looks like it must weigh fifty pounds, like her small frame can hardly hold it up but she's somehow managing.

"Brandi?" Tristan says, and wait a second...he *knows* her?

She folds herself into his arms, and he has to drop my hand in the process.

Are these the sorts of women he's friends with in Vegas?

Is it still a good idea for me to actually *move* here? He'll be here, and of course I want to be with him. I *need* to be with him, but I also trust him. I trust that he'll do right by me. He's never given me any reason *not* to trust him.

But Savannah's words about Tiffany rush back to me.

I suck in a breath.

He's left out some details. It's not anything for me to be upset about—after all, I've left out some pretty major details, too.

But what sort of marriage are we building if we're both entering it with secrets?

CHAPTER 19

Tristan

"This is my fiancée, Tessa," I say, pulling out of Brandi's rather tight embrace to awkwardly introduce the two women. "Tess, this is Brandi."

"Nice to meet you," Tessa says, reaching out a hand to shake hers.

"I know I look crazy, but I swear I dance professionally," Brandi says to Tessa with a giggle. "Sometimes we're asked to walk around the Strip in costume to advertise our show."

"Where do you perform?" Tessa asks.

"Fremont Street," she says. She turns toward me, and my heart races because I know what she's going to ask before she even asks it. "Will I see you at the club later?"

I shake my head just slightly. "We have plans."

She sticks out her bottom lip in a pout, and I shift on my feet as I try to find some way to escape this uncomfortable situation. I wasn't expecting to run into Brandi of all people just walking down the damn Strip.

"Too bad," she says. "Some of the guys there *really* like pregnant women." She lifts a shoulder and rolls her eyes. "It's a whole thing, you know?"

I clench my jaw as I try to come up with something to say to that. Tessa clearly has a question in her eyes, and I'm not quite sure how to answer it.

"Anyway, I need to get back to my girls," she says, nodding up ahead where we see more women in fruity headdresses and gold bikinis. "But you should stop by sometime this weekend. I've seen your boys around a lot lately." She winks as she walks away.

"Club?" Tessa asks the moment we're out of Brandi's earshot. "What club?"

I clear my throat.

We have literally been in Las Vegas three hours and this is already about to come out.

No secrets, right?

It's time to tell her the truth.

I lower my voice and lean in toward her as I grab her elbow and direct her back toward our hotel. "It's an exclusive club for, uh…for people who can afford it. Athletes, celebrities, millionaires. Let's get back to our room and I'll tell you more about it, okay?"

We haven't even been up to our room yet. Maybe that's the right place to tell her everything. Out here in the middle of the Strip surrounded by people, however, is *not* the right place, particularly given the nondisclosures we had to sign.

She gives me a strange look, but she just shakes her head and shrugs a little as if she doesn't get it but she'll go along with it.

We're almost back to the Venetian when we see a huge crowd of people at a standstill.

"What's going on?" Tessa asks. She moves to her tiptoes as she tries to get a peek, but I'm tall enough that I can see over most of the heads of the people here.

And when I spot who the crowd is circled around, I suck in a sharp breath.

What are the goddamn chances?

"Holy shit," she murmurs. "Is that Victor Bancroft?"

"Yep," I say, and I turn to leave.

She tugs my arm. "He's, like, my *favorite* actor! Number two on my list, only behind Ben Olson."

I freeze. "Excuse me?"

She tries again. "I mean behind Tristan Higgins?"

"Better, but still. Olson?" I ask.

She giggles. "You know what I mean. It's just a meaningless list."

"Uh, not really. Not when Ben Olson is one of my close friends and there's an actual shot you could meet him. Besides, he's *married*. He has kids," I say.

"You think that makes him less attractive?" She giggles, and I can't tell if she's just being silly or if I'm overreacting and about to pick a fight because I don't want to get into how I really know Brandi.

"Let's just backburner the list discussion for now, but I don't have a *list* and I don't think you should, either."

"It's just for fun," she says, and she almost seems a little hurt that I'd insinuate otherwise.

I lower my lips to her ear. "You're cruising for a punishment."

She squirms as her eyes connect with mine, and just at that moment Victor spots me through the parting of the crowd. "Tristan!" he says. He starts to move in our direction, but it's slow progress because of all the people.

And, of course, when he calls my name, everyone turns to look at *me*, and then I'm recognized as some of the throng moves in my direction.

I wasn't expecting this. I just wanted to take a walk down Las Vegas Boulevard with my fiancée to show her some of the most famous sights.

"Oh my God, you *know* him?" Tessa murmurs as he makes his way over to me.

Yeah, I know him. He's one of the owners of the club I'm a member of…but I can't exactly say that.

Someone asks me for a selfie, and then another and another, and I just keep taking them because what the hell else do you do when Victor Bancroft calls you out and is making his way over to you?

"Good to see you," he says, slapping my back. "You coming tonight?"

I shake my head, and *we're getting married* is on my lips, but I stop myself from saying it. We don't want it getting out to the press that we're here this weekend to get married, and telling Victor Bancroft in the middle of a throng of his fans that's why we're here would probably not be a well-kept secret.

Tessa lurches forward, and I grab her, slipping an arm around her waist. "I'm gonna take her back to our hotel before she gets pushed over," I tell Victor, and he nods.

"Good seeing you. Hope you'll stop by," he calls as we walk away.

People are following us, I'm sure of it, so we duck into a Walgreens.

"What are we doing?" Tessa asks. "And how do you know Victor Bancroft? What is this club?"

"I'll tell you everything later," I say in a hushed tone. "I'm just making sure nobody's following us up to our room."

We leave Walgreens and walk past the Venetian and over to a coffee shop on the other side, where I grab a quick cup. I think whoever might've been following us would have lost interest at this point, so I finally walk her back into the

No MISTAKE

Venetian. We walk through the maze of the casino to find our elevators, and then we head up to our suite.

I chose the presidential suite. You only get married once, after all—or twice, in my case, I guess—and I wanted the very finest accommodations for my bride.

Her jaw drops when she walks into the suite. She beelines straight for the window to check out the view. We're facing the Strip, and the Mirage is just to the left across the street. It's beautiful, and I glance around as I take in all the details of the room. Two couches, a bunch of wingback chairs, a fireplace, a large dining table with eight chairs…even a piano in one corner.

Tessa turns from the window and looks around the suite. "This is too much, Tristan."

"Nothing's too much for you," I say.

She shakes her head a little. "I'm a simple girl. I don't need all this fancy stuff. A room with a bed would've been just fine. You didn't have to spend all this—"

I hold up a hand. "I wanted to."

She sighs as if she's simply giving in, and she perches on one of the wingback chairs. She sinks a little more into it when she realizes how comfortable it is. "What's this club? And how do you know Victor Bancroft?"

I glance out the window and chew my bottom lip for a second as I try to figure out how to explain myself, and I decide to start at the beginning. "The day of your father's funeral, I had to get out of town fast because I had practice the next day. I got home and was ready to just call it a night when my ex-wife came in the room and just pissed me all the way off. A buddy had asked earlier if I wanted to go out, and I accepted the invitation. I went to his house, and a couple other guys I'm close to were already there. He asked us if we wanted to try a new kind of club that we hadn't been to before, and he wouldn't tell us anything about it until we signed nondisclosure agreements."

"Nondisclosure agreements?" she repeats.

I nod. "We basically had to agree not to tell anyone about the club. I'm not even supposed to be talking about it with you."

"What the hell kind of club is this?" she presses.

I suck in a breath as I turn my gaze to the window. "It's an exclusive place for people who can afford membership. The first floor is a basic nightclub. The second is an upscale gentleman's club. And the third floor…uh, the third floor is a place where people can explore sexuality in a safe, open environment."

"It's a…a…*sex* club?"

I stand and walk over to the window to look down over the Strip. "Yes." I turn around to face her, and I'm not sure I'll ever get that look of shock on her face out of my head. "Well, the third floor is. I didn't know exactly what I was getting into, and I went that first night out of curiosity mixed with peer pressure. I'd been fighting to get out of a divorce for two years, I saw you holding Cameron's hand at the funeral…I was in a bad place mentally, so I went."

"Just the one time?" she asks carefully.

I shake my head as I stare down at the floor with shame. "I became a member."

"Oh my God," she murmurs. "Did you…did you sleep with the bikini girl?"

"No!" I shake my head quickly. "No. I never slept with anybody there. I spent more time on the first floor than anywhere else. But Brandi and I became…friends."

She arches her brows as she folds her arms over her chest and settles back into her chair. "I'm supposed to believe you went to a sex club more than once to make friends and you never had sex at it?"

"It's the truth. And it's not *exclusively* a sex club. It's more of a members-only club where sex happens on the third floor."

"Why didn't you tell me?" she whispers.

"It never came up. It was just a different sort of club where I hung out a few times before we reconnected, and I was embarrassed that I went at all." I shrug. "Can you understand that?"

She shakes her head a little. "I...I'm not sure, Tristan. I feel like I don't know you at all right now." She purses her lips. "Did you spend much time on the third floor?"

I lift a shoulder. "Not a lot, but yeah, I did go there a few times."

"What did you do there if you weren't having sex?"

I clear my throat, hoping what I'm about to say isn't even worse than having sex. "I watched. Sometimes I provided aftercare."

She gives me a confused look. "Aftercare?"

"It's hard to define. In its most basic form, it's a way of checking in with somebody after they've had sex and making sure they've been taken care of both physically and emotionally," I say.

She wrinkles her nose, and it's clear she's disgusted by what I just confessed, as if she's picturing something that's not at all what it was really like. "So you cleaned up other people's messes?"

"No," I say, pushing hard not to get defensive over this. "It wasn't like that." I blow out a breath. "Brandi wanted to sleep with me. I didn't want to sleep with her, so I told her I'd watch her fuck somebody else." She winces at my language, but I continue. "She had sex with a guy and when it was over, he just walked out of the room. I felt bad—like it was because of me she slept with the first guy who agreed to after I told her to find somebody, and then he treated her like shit. So I handed her a washcloth to clean herself up. I talked to her and made sure she was okay."

"Did you kiss her?" she asks through gritted teeth.

I shake my head and turn toward the window, a sudden sadness sweeping through me. "I was never interested in her. Ever since you disappeared, all I've been trying to do is find somebody who makes me feel half the way you do, and nobody ever measured up. I've been trying to find myself for seven goddamn years, and no matter what I did, I was lost. It wasn't until you came back into my life that I found myself again."

She's quiet for a moment as she processes that. I expect some reciprocation, but that's not what comes out of her mouth at all.

"Is that what you were doing when you slept with Tiffany Gable right after I left? Trying to *find yourself?*"

Her voice is a low hiss, and fear filters through my veins.

I guess we're really doing this.

CHAPTER 20

Tessa

I didn't mean to hit him when he was already down, but I couldn't help the words as they flew out of my mouth.

A sex club?

Brandi?

Tiffany Gable?

I'm glad it's out in the open. I don't want secrets between us, and maybe this gives me permission to finally share my secret now, too.

Maybe we can both come clean and figure out how to move forward together.

I have no right to be angry that he kept secrets from me. I'd be a hypocrite to be angry for that.

God, even in a fucking *sex club* he went the route of swooping in as a hero with this aftercare nonsense. I've never met anybody with as big a savior complex as Tristan Higgins, and all this has done is set us back a few steps as I'm back to wondering whether he's with me because he wants to fix me.

I don't need fixing. I don't need saving.

I just want a partner.

"I didn't voluntarily sleep with her," he murmurs.

"Oh come off it," I spit. "Stop acting like a martyr."

He shakes his head. "I was beyond wasted, Tess. I don't remember a second of my night with her. All I remember is that I was trying to numb the pain from you leaving. I thought about driving to the Quad Cities to find that guy Robbie, the one Kevin Harkins always talked about who sold drugs. I thought about getting high. I thought about risking my entire future with something, anything that would take away an ounce of the pain I was feeling after you left. Tiff knew that. She sat with me while I cried over you, and then she took advantage of it. Of *me*. A few weeks later she claimed she was pregnant."

"Was she?" I ask.

I shake my head. "She didn't keep good track of her cycle and she got her period a few days later. I honestly can't even confirm I ever slept with her. I blacked out that night."

"Why didn't you tell me that?" I ask. "Why are we keeping so many secrets from each other?" The words are out before I can stop them. I just admitted I'm keeping secrets, too, but he's the one on the hot seat.

Luckily he glosses over my words.

"I couldn't think of any good reason to tell you. Something happened that I have no memory of seven years ago." He shrugs. "It's not exactly breaking news, and I didn't want you to be hurt by it."

I think about that for a beat. Would telling him about the baby my dad made me give up change anything? Or would it only hurt us both?

"Would you have ever told me if I hadn't brought it up?" I ask.

Maybe I'm looking for a reason not to make things harder between the two of us.

"I don't know." His brows dip. "Wait a minute. How did you know about it?"

No MISTAKE

"Your ex-wife," I admit. "She called me not so long ago trying to get me to leave you."

"Fuck her," he mutters. "Why didn't you tell me she called you?"

I don't have an answer to that, but I do need to tell him something, too.

It's time to come clean.

I draw in a deep breath as I try to gather the courage to tell him about my history, too—the history that involves him. I sway like a pendulum back and forth as I try to determine whether he should know, and right now I'm swinging in the *tell him* area. "As long as we're sharing secrets, I have something I need to say to you, too."

His brows draw together.

"When my dad put me in that car to go to my aunt's house in Chicago, it wasn't so I could finish high sch—"

Our hotel room phone starts ringing—*loudly*—interrupting my train of thought.

I glance over at the phone. "Who even knows we're here?"

He shrugs and moves across the room to answer it. "Hello?" I listen to his side of the brief conversation, and when he hangs up, he blows out a breath. "It was the chapel welcoming us to the hotel and letting me know that the chapel is open now if we'd like to come take a look at the room where we're getting married." He pauses and glances up at me. "Assuming we're still getting married."

The moment has passed, and I'm not sure whether to be grateful or devastated. I wanted to tell him, but I'm also glad for the interruption.

I sigh, and then I stand and cross the room toward him. "Of course we're still getting married," I say softly. I reach my fingertips to the scruff on his jaw. "I'm glad you told me. I don't think less of you because you went to that club. You shouldn't be ashamed of what you did. If it made you feel good, or made you forget your pain, or made you happy…it's not shameful. I grew up in a house where sex wasn't talked about, where it was shameful and wrong, and I don't want to raise my daughter in the same sort of environment. And it starts here." I shrug. "I'm not saying it's okay for her to go to a sex club, just to be clear."

He chuckles.

"But what I am saying is that if you were in a safe and consensual environment and you found your place there, it's nothing to be ashamed of." His eyes meet mine, and I wiggle my brows suggestively. "And if you ever want to take me there and introduce me to all the other celebrities…"

"Oh no you don't," he says, and he grabs me into his arms as we both laugh. "You're all mine, Tessa Taylor."

"And you're all mine, too, Tristan Higgins."

His lips lower to mine.

"Wait a minute…" I begin. I pull back from him and narrow my eyes. "Is that where you picked up the whole *punishment* thing?"

He raises his brows and smiles. "I might've picked up a trick or two there."

He proves it then as clothes start flying off in every direction, and we have a super-fast quickie where he bends me over the side of the bed since he promised we'd be at the chapel shortly.

I guess my confession will have to wait a little longer.

We get dressed afterward and head down the elevator, and I'm in awe of everything around me on the entire walk over. When we get to the chapel where we're getting married, a wave of destiny washes over me.

Ironic since it's the Destiny chapel…but it's perfect.

No **MISTAKE**

It's simple and elegant, a white and bright small room with chairs set up facing a doorway where we'll stand to be married in two days. Gorgeous white floral arrangements are situated around the room, and two huge floor vases serve to hold back curtains from the doorway.

A woman rushes into the room. "Tristan?" she asks, and he nods. She turns to me with a smile. "And Tessa. I'm Gloria."

"Nice to meet you," I say, and I reach over to shake her outstretched hand.

"And you," she says formally, shaking Tristan's hand next. "I'm your event coordinator. This is our Destiny chapel overlooking the gardens. We have seating for up to forty guests, and you'll have exclusive use of this room plus photo and floral allowances with your package. We provide an officiant if needed, and there will be a thirty-minute rehearsal tomorrow afternoon should you require one. Do you have your marriage license?"

"Not yet," Tristan says. "I was planning to take Tessa tomorrow."

She nods. "They're still open if you'd like to get it tonight. It's always nice to have that time bumper if you can fit it in."

She goes over more details, and I start to glaze over as it all quickly becomes overwhelming.

My brain is stuck on *marriage license*.

That makes it real.

Standing in the chapel holding Tristan's hand while she goes over the details should make it real, but a marriage license is a tangible sign that we're really doing this.

If someone would've told me a year ago when I was a single nurse sharing an apartment with my best friend in Chicago pining over my lost love and blaming my father for everything wrong in my life that this is where I'd be standing a mere three hundred sixty-five days later, I never would've believed it.

Yet here we are.

I'm pregnant, I'm about to marry Tristan Higgins—who's a member of some sort of sex club, we own the house on the corner in Fallon Ridge, and I'm moving to Vegas to live with Luke and Ellie Dalton while we get settled.

I feel like I'm dreaming, like I'm floating on a cloud as Gloria takes us on a tour of the gardens at the Venetian, where we'll take our wedding photographs after the ceremony.

I'm still floating as she takes me into a bridal suite to show me a selection of gowns. Big ones and small ones, long, and short, white and cream and even a black one, lacy and silky…there are dozens to choose from, and I pick the first one on the rack.

I slip into it, and I immediately know it's perfect.

What a life. I feel blessed beyond measure.

Which is why I'm so completely blindsided when it all comes crumbling down.

CHAPTER 21

Tessa

It's a little after five o'clock Vegas time when I wake on Thursday morning. It's the day before I'm getting married, and I'm warm in my fiancé's arms.

Time changes are weird, but I'm wide awake and ready to face the day. I take a shower, and Tristan's sitting up in bed scrolling his phone when I emerge already dressed.

He twists his lips as he looks at me. "I was hoping you'd come out naked."

I giggle. "I think we're supposed to wait to have sex until we're married. Right?"

"Depends which source you're referencing. I've heard staying together the night before the wedding is bad luck, but I've never heard it's bad luck to have a nice round of morning sex the day before."

"Sorry to tell you this, buddy, but that quickie before the chapel yesterday was your last sex as a single man." I set my hand on my hip.

He gets out of bed and stalks over to me in just his boxers, and I stare at his body for a beat. God, he's hot.

And he's *mine*. After everything that's happened, everything we've been through…he's mine.

He takes me in his arms, and I get the feeling it's going to be hard to stick to my guns on this one. He thrusts his hips to mine, and speaking of hard…

"I'll go take a cold shower," he mutters.

I laugh as he heads into the bathroom. I grab my phone off the nightstand and settle into the chair by the window while I wait for Tristan. I see I have a few new messages that came through when I was asleep.

I open the first one, and it's from Savannah.

Savannah: *Heard you're in Vegas and marrying Tristan this weekend. Didn't I warn you about that?*

My chest tightens and my stomach twists as fear filters through me.

How does she know we're here? How does she know we're getting married?

I nearly hop up to interrupt Tristan, but I can wait until he gets out of the shower.

I lift my eyes to the window and look out over the view. The sun's not up yet, but the sky is starting to get bright. My stomach rumbles with hunger, but I'm in my third trimester of pregnancy. I'm always hungry.

I hear Tristan's phone buzz over on the nightstand and wonder whether Savannah is texting him, too. I want to check, but I don't. I won't be that girl that sneaks peeks at her man's phone.

I trust him.

He walks through the room with a towel tied around his waist a few minutes later, his hair wet and slicked back and his muscles shimmering as he moves through the room toward his suitcase. I sit back, totally distracted by his body as I watch the show for a second before I remember the text.

"Savannah texted me," I say.

"Just now?"

No MISTAKE

I shake my head. "When we were asleep. I just saw it now."

"What did it say?"

I open my phone and read him the message. "Heard you're in Vegas and marrying Tristan this weekend. Didn't I warn you about that?" I glance up at him. "How does she know that? We haven't told anybody. We haven't even gotten our marriage license yet."

His brows draw together, and he runs a hand through his hair. "It's her gift. She slithers her way in and has people everywhere. She's probably got somebody at the airport who spotted us, or maybe she knows Gloria from the chapel. She'll stop at nothing to get what she wants."

"And she wants *you*." I press my lips together.

"She can't have me," he murmurs, walking over to me and wrapping his arms around me. He smells like shower gel, and a needy ache presses between my thighs.

I literally just said we need to wait until after we're married tomorrow.

We can do this. I don't have to get him naked every time we're in the same room together.

Even though I want to.

God, this is a weird stage of pregnancy.

"I don't know if she wants me so much as she doesn't want anybody else to have me," he admits. He turns toward his suitcase. He pulls off his towel and tosses it over a chair next to him, and I'm treated to a lovely view of his naked backside. I stare as he reaches into his bag, pulls out some boxers, and steps into them.

He turns back toward me and chuckles at the expression on my face. "See something you like?"

I blink as I try to shake it off. "Yes, but we're in the middle of a crisis."

He laughs. "Savannah isn't a crisis. She's a headache, but I won't give her much more credit than that."

My stomach rumbles again.

"Let me finish up and we can grab breakfast, okay?" He presses his lips to my cheek on his way by. "Don't worry about her. We'll be married tomorrow before she can do anything to stop us."

I hold those words close to my heart, hoping he's right. But somehow, I know he's not.

We eat breakfast, and when we're done, we head downtown to get our marriage license.

All we need is the officiant to name us husband and wife, and we'll be official.

Does any little girl grow up dreaming of a quickie Vegas wedding?

I didn't.

But does every little girl dream of the perfect partner standing at the end of the aisle waiting for her?

I did.

From the moment I met him, the face in those dreams was always Tristan. My dreams are *literally* coming true right before my eyes.

And I won't let his evil ex-wife be the one who pinches me to wake me up from it.

CHAPTER 22

Tessa

We walk around downtown a little before we take a car back to the hotel. "Once you live here, we can take our time touring the sights," he says, my hand clutched firmly in his in the backseat.

"Can't wait," I murmur. We'll have a baby then, and life will be different. But that's life, right? A series of transitions, and we fumble our way through from one to the next, doing the best we can with what we have.

He squeezes my hand. "I thought about swinging by Luke and Ellie's so you could see where we'll be staying when we first move back out here, but I don't think we have much time to kill since our parents will be getting here around lunch time."

I glance over at him. "You still want to do that?"

"Move in with Luke?" he asks.

I nod.

"I think it makes sense to make plans to stay somewhere temporary at least until the ink is dry on the fifth-year extension, which should be any day now, but I don't want you to move out here and feel all alone. I think it's a great idea to stay with someone I trust, someone who can help with the baby when I'll be away at camp in July and then in season through January."

"And maybe February," I say, offering a smile as I hint that I expect him to win the Super Bowl.

He chuckles. "With any luck. But I don't like talking about it." He wrinkles his nose. "It feels like a jinx, you know?"

I nod. "Do you have any other superstitions?"

He laughs. "All players do. It's a game of rituals, and if something works one time, you stick with it until it grows into this huge thing that must be done at all costs or we will lose. Some guys don't shave when we're on a winning streak. Some wear the same shoelaces to every game. One guy won't sit during a game—he has to stand when he's not on the field. Another guy will only drink orange Gatorade. Some guys do yoga before a game. But me? I take a lap around the field to center myself before a game."

"You run?" I ask.

He nods. "I focus on the markers and try to learn the field since every single one feels unique in its own way, like it's a slightly different surface even if it's the same physical material. So I run a lap, feel the grass or the turf under my shoes, breathe in the air, and force my mind to focus on the game and making plays."

The car turns into the driveway at the Venetian, so we're almost back. "Both home and away games?" I ask.

"Yep," he says, and the car pulls behind some traffic, so we wait our turn for the driver to pull up so we can get out. "I did it a time or two in high school but it wasn't a ritual or anything. When we started playing big games in college, that's when I felt like I needed a lap to get the nervous energy out. And it just evolved from there."

We move forward, and we thank our driver before getting out. Tristan holds out a hand to help me, and when I glance up after closing the door behind me, I'm shocked at who I see standing on the sidewalk.

No **MISTAKE**

"Sara?" I squeal as I rush over to her and squeeze her.

She grins at me. "I wasn't about to miss my best friend's wedding!"

"I can't believe you're really here!" We dance around with excitement. I told her about the wedding, told her I wanted her there…but I didn't know if she'd actually be able to make it.

"I'm Tristan," he says to her, and she giggles nervously.

"Wow," she says, staring up at him. He's a tall drink of water, but he's also gorgeous and he's an NFL star. It's a pretty common reaction.

I smack her playfully in the arm. "Hands off, sister. He's mine."

"I can't believe you never mentioned your history with him," she says.

Tristan glances at me, a question in his eyes.

I shrug a little awkwardly. "It was too painful to bring it up when I thought it was long over. And then we found each other again. Happy ending." I grin, though the thought that we're not actually *at* the ending crosses my mind.

She grabs the handle of the suitcase beside her I hadn't noticed. "I need to go check in," she says, and we walk into the hotel with her.

"Where's Shane?" I ask.

"He had to work today and tomorrow so he won't be coming out, but I called in sick and figured we could have a huge bachelorette party." She winks as she glances at my stomach, clearly teasing me.

Tristan chuckles, too. "I actually have plans for a bachelor-slash-bachelorette party tonight."

My brows arch. "You do?"

He lifts a shoulder. "I'm full of surprises."

We're still in the lobby when Sue, Russ, and my mom walk through the front doors. Sue and Russ look like they've been here before, but my mom just stares around the place with awe in her eyes—much like I did when I first got here. Much like I still am, I suppose.

I run over to my mom—well, *run* might be a bit of an exaggeration with fifteen extra pounds all in my stomach—and squeeze her before hugging both Tristan's parents.

"We're so excited to be here," Sue says. "We just couldn't be happier for you and Tristan."

Tears heat behind my eyes. She always made me feel like I was a part of their family, but now I actually will be.

It all feels so surreal.

After everyone gets settled, we all head out to lunch at a restaurant in our hotel, and then we all head over to the chapel. We show off the room where we'll be married, we meet with Gloria to finalize all the details, and I show the ladies the dress I chose.

My mom cries, and so does Sue.

It's becoming more and more real, and I can't wait to marry Tristan tomorrow.

CHAPTER 23

Tristan

It might not be a traditional bachelor party, but I don't need the strippers and a big event. Ben threw me the Big D Bash, and that was a good enough blowout for me.

Tonight is about celebrating with our families, and tomorrow will be more of that as we join them together as one. Travis came out to dinner with us, too, and my mom gave him a bag of puppy chow that she brought all the way from Iowa.

And with family in mind, I rented a private room in a restaurant in our hotel. It's tucked away and has a door so we can celebrate and talk and enjoy our time without anybody questioning why we're here or coming up to Travis and me for autographs.

It's a perfect night filled with laughter and love, and my future wife positively glows beside me. She's worn out after the excitement of the day, and she's ready to head up. She's staying in our suite tonight, while I got a different room. Tomorrow she'll be pampered all day in our suite with our moms and her maid of honor before I meet her in the chapel to marry her.

I hold her in my arms outside the elevator before she heads up to bed, and I press a soft kiss to her lips. "I'll see you at the wedding," I say softly.

The smile that lights up her face reminds me why we're doing this.

"I'll be the one in the white dress," she teases.

"I'll be the one waiting anxiously to marry you." I kiss her again, and then the elevator doors open. "Goodnight."

"Night," she says, and she stands on the elevator alone. Our eyes are connected, and she lifts a hand to wave before the doors slide closed.

I blow out a breath. In less than twenty-four hours, and she'll be my wife, and just like that, all the pain and mistakes of the past will wash away as we embark on our new life together.

If only it were that simple.

If only things ever went to plan.

"Coax?" a voice behind me suggests, and I chuckle as I turn around to face Travis.

"Not tonight, my friend." I shake my head.

"Yeah, I figured as much. You keeping your membership?" he asks.

I shrug. "I told Tessa about it. I was sort of forced into it when I ran into Brandi walking down the Strip."

He huffs out a chuckle. "Small goddamn world, isn't it?"

"We saw Victor, too. Apparently he tops the list of celebrities my bride wants to fuck." My tone is dry as the conversation comes back to me.

Travis wrinkles his nose. "I would've thought it would be you."

"I don't think I count, but Olson made the list."

He laughs and slaps me on the back. "Honeys, then?"

I shake my head.

"It's the night before your wedding. It's bad luck not to see titties bouncing all over the place the night before your wedding." He goes for a convincing tone.

No MISTAKE

"I've never heard that particular superstition," I admit. "I wouldn't say no to some whiskey and blackjack, though."

"Deal," he says, and he tosses out a hand for me to shake.

I spot my parents and Tessa's mom as they walk toward the casino floor, and they see me at the same time. My dad decides to join Travis and me, and my mom and Tessa's mom hang out by the slots.

We head toward the high limit lounge in this place, and we sit at a table.

We order some whiskey, we spend a shitload of money, and we get fucked up as we laugh, play cards, and drink and drink and drink.

My dad can't keep up with the two of us—neither in the amount of money we're playing nor the amount of whiskey we're consuming—and he heads over to meet my mom after a while. Presumably they head up to bed shortly after that.

Travis and I focus on cards and whiskey, and I find the more I drink, the more money I toss onto the table. I win some, I lose some, but the whiskey is a constant.

Some woman approaches Travis after we've been playing-slash-drinking for a couple hours, and he seems to know her. She watches us play a while, and I see her hand slide under the table. It doesn't take a genius to figure out where their night is headed.

He asks me if it's okay for him to take off with her. I'm not one to cock-block, so I decide to call it a night.

All in all, it was exactly what I wanted out of a "bachelor party." If I had my choice, I'd have Jaxon, Cory, Austin, Patrick, and Deon here, too, and maybe the rest of the wide receivers, but it's short notice and it's supposed to be a secret.

They can be there when we celebrate in a year from now after the season's over, after she's had the baby, after we're more settled in and she falls in love with Vegas the same way I have.

I'm about to head up to my room and call it a night when a voice stops me in my tracks. "Tristan, wait."

I shouldn't wait. I shouldn't listen to what she has to say. I should get on the elevator and go up to my room and pretend I never heard her.

But I'm just drunk enough that I stop. I turn around.

I face her. "What are you doing here?"

"Are you here to get married?" Brandi asks me.

"Yes, I am. Why do you ask?" If I was completely sober, I might've been smart enough to either lie or play off her question with a non-answer, but that's not where I find myself.

"Where's the bride to be?" she asks, ignoring my question.

"Sleeping."

"Want to go somewhere and have some fun while you're still single?" she practically purrs in my ear.

I shake my head.

"Are you one of those guys who doesn't care if you're single or married? You'll take it any way you can get it?" she asks.

I laugh. "No. That doesn't sound anything like me at all, to be honest."

"But weren't you married when you joined Coax?" she asks.

"I was, and you might've noticed I never had sex in the club," I point out.

"I think the other things you did there would offend some women." She shrugs. "Your girl seems…vanilla. Is that what you want?" The way she says that word, *vanilla*, makes it sound like a terrible thing.

"What she is or isn't is none of your business," I hiss.

She taps her chin. "Oh, that's so funny you say that, because it sort of actually *is* my business."

My brows dip. "How?"

No **MISTAKE**

She lifts a shoulder, and then she blows me a kiss and winks as she starts to walk away. "You'll find out soon."

Her parting words just aren't good enough.

I walk after her and grab her shoulder, spinning her around to face me. "What do you have planned, Brandi?" My tone comes out a little more desperate than I mean for it to.

She doesn't answer.

"Why are you doing this?" I whisper.

"Why does anybody do anything?" She pulls her arm out of my grasp and stalks away from me, leaving me to ponder that question.

As I step onto the elevator, her words play on repeat in my mind.

Why does anybody do anything?

Love, money, and fear.

Those are the three biggest motivators in the world.

I scratch out love immediately.

Is somebody paying her to do whatever it is she's doing? She tends to run with an elite group that could afford to. Maybe that's what she's after.

Fear? Is somebody threatening her? I have no way of knowing.

My brain returns to love.

Is she in love with me? That's a ridiculous notion. Maybe somebody she loves is trying to get to me for some reason. Or maybe...

Maybe it's not as ridiculous as I first thought.

After all, she came onto me the first time we met. I tried to politely decline, but she did things I asked her to do. Does she have feelings for me? Does she think whatever it is she's planning will make me run from Tessa to her?

I sigh.

Thank God we're doing this tomorrow. I'm so damn tired of people working so hard against us. It won't stop when we're married, and I'm smart enough to know that.

A piece of paper is a piece of paper, and it doesn't change much…except it does, and having been married once already, I have firsthand experience at exactly how much it does change. Savannah made sure I'd know, and it took me two years to ignite that piece of paper into flames.

Once we've made that lifelong vow—because with Tessa, it *will* be lifelong—then we have the insurance of commitment. We both have that reason to hang on even when someone else tries to do their worst to us. We'll have that vow we made pulling us back toward each other instead of taking the easy way out.

Even though I know I'm going to a different room than the penthouse I stayed in with her last night, for just a split second after I slide the keycard in and open the door to an empty room, a bolt of fear lances through me.

It's empty because she's in a different room. My brain knows that, but I still feel that same anxiety I did the day she left me.

Is this a mistake? Are we rushing into things? Do we need more time to plan, to dream, to have everything exactly the way we want it? For her to have the baby so we can adjust to our new life? For her to be with me through an entire season to see if it's even the life she really wants? What if love isn't enough?

I wish I hadn't had so much whiskey.

These thoughts and fears that plague me…they wouldn't be here if I hadn't had so much to drink or if I'd have gone up to my room a few minutes earlier or even if I would've just stayed down there playing a little longer after Travis left. Or maybe Brandi was waiting around all night for me to get on that elevator so she could put doubts and fears into my mind.

No MISTAKE

And if fear is a motivator…well, maybe it's a good think I drank as much as I did.

Because if I wasn't about to pass out, I'm not quite sure what my fears might motivate me to do.

CHAPTER 24

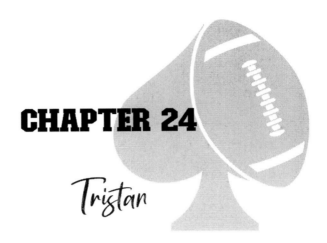

Tristan

The sun is up, the birds are chirping—I assume, since the windowpanes in this place are thick and block out most of the noise outside—and I have one hell of a brutal hangover.

How much fucking whiskey did I drink last night?

Only God, and maybe the server, knows the answer to that.

It's my wedding day, and my dad asked if we could start the day with eighteen holes at my favorite course. As I force myself into the shower, feeling like I'm carrying my pounding head separately from the rest of my body, I have regrets about the six-thirty tee time.

I didn't drink enough to black out. I remember every detail of my night, including the run-in with Brandi before I took the elevator up. Maybe it's a good thing I drank as much as I did since otherwise, I would've tossed and turned all night trying to figure out what the fuck she was talking about.

I'll find out soon. That's what she told me.

I don't know what she has planned, but I just pray it doesn't interfere with the wedding.

I have a sinking feeling it will, though.

I meet my dad in the hotel lobby at six, and he laughs when he sees me.

"Feeling a little rough this morning, kid?" he asks. He's holding two coffees and a bag, and he hands me a coffee.

"Thanks," I say with a shrug. "I'm all right."

He hands me a small package, and it's warm and feels like food. "This should help."

I unwrap it and chuckle when I see what's inside. A breakfast burrito filled with greasy bacon, sausage, eggs, and fried potatoes.

"This is perfect, Dad. How did you know?"

"I know you well enough to guess you stayed out late with your buddy and you two probably drank way too much. Nothing cures a hangover quite like greasy food and coffee."

I think of Ben's concoction at the Big D Bash and wish I had a pitcher of that dog shit right now, but my dad's solution will work, too.

"Oh," he says, reaching into his pocket. He pulls out a little packet of ibuprofen. "Your mom said to give you this, too."

I laugh as I sling an arm around my dad. "You two are the best."

And then I unsling my arm and take the pills.

Since my car is back in Iowa, we grab a Lyft to the course. It's the same course we played last time, and as we wait for our turn on the second tee after I kicked my dad's ass on the first hole, I glance over at him, and he's staring at me thoughtfully.

"I know it's coming…so is this where you tell me that the key to a good marriage is communication?" I ask.

He chuckles. "Nah," he says. "It is, but that's not what I want to say to you today."

"Then what?"

"Look at how you took that first hole. You caught a birdie while I bogeyed. Sports have always come easy for you. You hit homeruns in baseball. You slam dunked in basketball. You nearly always scored under par in golf. And you made it all the way to the NFL, where you're seeing your dreams come to life before you. I'm proud of you, kiddo."

"Thanks, Dad," I manage around the emotion clogging my throat. I feel oddly choked up at his speech. I swallow thickly as I wait for him to get to the inevitable *but*.

"And now you're taking on a wife and a baby. It's a lot. Kids are hard work." He elbows me. "Believe me."

I laugh.

"But absolutely and totally worth it. Believe me on that one, too."

It's our turn to tee off, so he doesn't get to the *but*. Yet.

I hit right down the center of the course, and he slices right. "I don't know where you get your athleticism from," he mutters as we both slide back into the cart to find our balls.

I laugh, and we finish the hole before we meet back up in the cart to wait for the third tee.

"I'm waiting for you to drop the hammer," I say.

His brows draw together. "The hammer?"

"The *but*. You're feeding me the good stuff, and it's nice to hear, but I feel like it's coming with a warning."

He presses his lips together and shakes his head wryly as he looks out over the course ahead of us. He glances back at me. "Athletic, good-looking, and smart as a whip, too. Lucky kid."

I settle back into the driver's seat to prepare for his words. "Well, let's get on with it."

"Did you ever find out what happened when she left the first time?" he asks.

I shake my head.

"Did you tell her about Tiffany Gable?"

I nod as I suck my bottom lip between my teeth and chew a little nervously.

"So you've given her your honesty, but she hasn't returned that?"

I blow out a breath. "I told her the past didn't matter, and I'm choosing to believe the story she and her family told is the truth," I finally say.

He holds up his hands. "And that's certainly a fine choice, son. Like I said, athletics have always come easy for you. But not everything in life is quite that easy, as you found out when you married that ex-wife of yours. I just want you to be happy, and I want you to be fully sure you know what you're getting into."

"I appreciate the concern, Dad, but I know. I've known since I was twelve." My voice is blunt.

He squeezes my knee. "I know you have. But don't you think you're rushing this?"

I lift a shoulder. "Maybe, but we both want this. I want to do it before the season starts. She wants to do it before the baby gets here. There are other factors at play," I say, remembering his words about me not treating him like he's dying, which forces me to choose not to mention another reason we're rushing this along. "We're both so goddamn tired of these forces constantly coming at us to break us apart."

"Marriage isn't going to fix that. Marriage isn't going to change who you are and suddenly make you invisible. Did it stop anyone from hitting on you when you were married to Savannah?" he asks.

"No," I admit. "And I know it won't fix anything, or change anything, but then we'll both have a vow to cling to when times get tough." I lower my voice as I stare out over the green grass. "She won't disappear on me again because she'll be tethered to our commitment."

"Is that what this is about? You're marrying her because you're afraid she'll walk away again if you don't?" he asks.

I shake my head. "No. I'm marrying her because I love her." I blow out a breath, and then I turn to look at him as I decide

No **MISTAKE**

to give him the whole truth. "I want you there, Dad. I want you standing next to me as my best man. It's important to me you stand up as a witness when I marry the woman I will spend the rest of my life with."

He presses his lips together again, and then he stares out over the grass, too. I wonder what he's thinking. I wonder if he's scared. I wonder if he's as scared to leave me as I am to lose him.

I push the negative thought away as I focus on the positive. He's here now, and I'll take him for as long as I'm allowed to keep him.

He squeezes my knee. "Okay, then. I will be there at five o'clock ready to stand by your side."

CHAPTER 25

It's been about as lowkey a day as I could hope for. Tristan thought of everything—the day started with massages and whatever other services we wanted at the hotel spa. We followed that up with manicures and pedicures, and now I'm sitting in a chair as someone does my make-up. My hair is next, and then it's time for the dress, pictures, and walking down the aisle toward my future.

"When I got engaged at Christmas, did you ever imagine you'd be walking down the aisle before me?" Sara asks me as Tonia, the make-up artist, sweeps eye shadow across my lids.

I chuckle without moving. "Never. And certainly not to the boy I'd thought I'd lost forever."

"It just really goes to show you how much you two are meant to be together forever," Sara says, and I hear someone approaching but I can't see who since my eyes are closed.

"I couldn't agree more." My mom's voice is calm and comforting.

Tonia finished my make-up, and she has me check the mirror.

"It's gorgeous," I say, shocked at how beautiful I feel even at seven months pregnant.

Tonia moves onto Sara next, and my mom and I head into the main living area of the suite.

"Can we talk for a minute?" she asks as we both walk over toward the window and sit in the wingback chairs overlooking the view.

"Of course," I say.

She takes my hand in hers as she ignores the view to study me. "Are you doing okay?"

I press my lips into a smile. "I'm doing better than I've ever been in my life."

Her lips lift into a smile, too. "That makes me so happy, honey. I just want you to know that not all men are like Cameron Foster or like your father. Some men are like Tristan. He's a good guy, and I'm just so pleased for you that you found each other again."

"Thanks, Mom," I say softly.

"It won't be without its hardships. No marriage is, but with him in the spotlight, too, you'll have an added layer of something I have zero experience with. But I have a little secret that helped me through many dark nights, and I'd like to share it with you if you'd like to hear it."

I nod as my brows knit together in total curiosity over what she's about to tell me.

"There were times I was angry with your father." She averts her eyes to the window and then back to me. "There were times I hated him. And, of course, there were good times, too. Everyone says don't go to bed angry, but the truth of it is that sometimes you will. And on those nights, or in the heat of an argument, or in those lonely dark moments when he's away, be sure to always ask yourself if the life you've built together is worth it. If the answer is yes, then you fight like hell to make it work. If even a single doubt creeps in that the answer is no…then you walk away. You only get one life, but that

No MISTAKE

doesn't mean you only get one shot to be as happy as you deserve."

"Did you ever have doubts about you and Dad?" I ask.

"Every single day from the time he sent you to his sister's house in Chicago up until the day he died," she admits, and tears heat behind my eyes. She shakes her head and bites her lip as she gets emotional, too. "Don't cry, honey. Don't ruin your make-up, but I feel like I need to say this. I wish I wouldn't have stayed. I thought I was doing the right thing, being a good example by sustaining a failed marriage, but I wasn't."

The look on my face must betray my emotions. Why the hell is she telling me this mere hours before I walk down the aisle?

And then it hits me just as she voices it, and just like that, I understand what Christine Foster was doing on my front porch not so long ago.

She was fighting like hell even though she knew it was a losing battle.

"I didn't marry a Tristan, honey," she says. "I married a Cameron who never cared about my feelings, who just did what he wanted. He never tried to make me happy. But I see the way Tristan is with you, and I see how you are with him. Just remember that the foundation of a strong marriage is honesty, so make sure you're always honest with him…about *everything*. When the time is right, of course."

I widen my eyes toward the next room. Sara doesn't know the *everything* she's referring to, and she nods as if she understands what I'm getting at.

"I love you, sweetheart," she says, and I lean over in my chair to give her an awkward sit-down hug.

"I love you, too, Mom," I say.

A knock at the door interrupts us.

I stand and squeeze her hand. "Thanks for saying all that."

I make my way to the door, and I throw it open after checking who's behind it.

"Happy wedding day!" Ellie says, and she practically leaps at me for a hug.

I giggle. "Thank you."

"Tristan invited us. I hope that's okay," she says. She snaps my photo. "You look gorgeous, and someone needed some BTS pics for the 'gram."

"BTS? Gram?" my mom echoes behind me.

"Hi Mrs. Taylor," Ellie says with a wave.

"Good to see you again, honey," she says, and I realize they must have met during the craft fair, but I was so busy running around that day I wasn't the one who made the introductions.

"BTS means *behind the scenes*," I clarify.

"And the 'gram is Instagram," Ellie says.

"Ah," my mom says, raising her brows. "Well, I'll leave you to it. I need to run back to my room to get dressed, but I'll be back shortly," my mom says.

"If you want hair or make-up, the girls are in the bathroom," I say.

"I'd love make-up," she says. "I ran out the door and did mascara in the car on the way here."

I laugh. It's so *Ellie* of her.

"Tessa?" someone calls from the bathroom, and I think it's June, the hair girl. "Your turn for hair!"

"You heard the lady," I say, and we both laugh as we march toward the bathroom for more pampering.

An hour later, it takes both Ellie and Sara to help me into my dress. My mom takes pictures as Sara laces up the back, and then everyone backs up as I stand in front of the mirror checking out the final product.

No **MISTAKE**

The dress I chose neither highlights nor hides my baby bump. I went with a high-waisted white dress with lace three-quarter sleeves and lace detail that extends over the low neckline and onto the bodice of the dress. It flows beautifully down to my feet, which are currently snug in a white pair of Keds for comfort, and I both look and feel like I stepped right out of a fairy tale.

"Oh my goodness," my mom breathes as she stares at me in the mirror from behind. "You are the most beautiful, glowing bride I've ever seen." She swipes at a tear.

I can't help a small giggle. "The glow is from the pregnancy sweats."

She offers a little laugh, too, and she squeezes my arm. "Tristan is one lucky boy."

"I'm one lucky girl," I murmur.

"A match made in heaven," Sara says.

Ellie grins. "Now let's get you two married."

"Deal." I glance at the clock. "Perfect timing for photos. Can you check to be sure Tristan is locked away in a room somewhere so he doesn't see me before the ceremony?" I ask.

"I'm on it," Ellie says, pulling out her phone to make a call. She confirms that Luke is with Tristan and they aren't anywhere near the chapel, so I draw in a deep breath, I take a few sips of water to calm my racing heart, and we make our way down.

CHAPTER 26

Tristan

"She's en route to the chapel for pre-ceremony photos," Luke tells me.

I glance at myself in the mirror. The last time I wore a tuxedo was to prom my junior year. I opted out my senior year since there was nobody I wanted to go with if it wasn't Tessa.

I didn't wear one when I married Savannah. It was a split-second decision on New Year's Eve. We were on the Strip, and she suggested it, and I was drunk enough to agree. I didn't have any better options and I had a good feeling that being connected to a respected journalist like her was a smart move.

That just tells you how stupid alcohol can make you.

I blow out a breath.

"It's getting real, huh?" Luke says, slapping me on the back.

I nod. "Were you nervous when you married Ellie?"

He chuckles. "When I married Ellie, I was in Hawaii on a family vacation, and she was marrying me as a business transaction. But yes, I was nervous as fuck…mostly because I was already in love with her, but I was fighting hard against it."

I've heard snippets of their story before, but never so candidly from Luke.

"And when you married Savannah?" I press.

He nods. "I felt like it was the wrong decision from the start, particularly since she was my brother's ex—girlfriend, but I didn't let that stop me. Are you nervous now?"

I press my lips together and lift my eyes to the window. I shake my head. "No. I'm not. And that feels weird—like I *should* be nervous but I'm not."

He moves in behind me and pats me on the shoulder. "I think that just means you're making the right choice."

"Thanks, man. I should've listened to your advice when I was with Savannah."

He shrugs. "Eh, live and learn, right?"

The door opens, and Travis walks in with my dad trailing behind him. Both are carrying tumblers filled with whiskey.

"To the groom," Travis says, handing me a cup. My dad hands Luke one, too, and we all toast.

"To the groom," the others echo, and we touch glasses before I chug the entire glass.

Okay, so maybe I'm a *little* nervous.

Not about marrying Tessa, obviously. I'm nervous about what could go wrong between now and an hour from now.

And as it turns out, I was right to be worried about it.

Every knock on my door sets me on edge.

The first time, it's my mom. The next time, it's Ellie. The pictures of the women are done. It's my turn.

I head down to the chapel and smile with my dad, with Travis, with Luke, with my mom, with both my parents.

The photos afterward will have my bride in them, and I just want the time to pass a little faster so we can get on with this.

We're ready.

Let's fucking go.

Let's do this.

No **MISTAKE**

The minutes seem like hours as the clock ticks toward five o'clock, like we're just allowing enough time and space for something to go wrong. Why didn't we plan this ceremony for four? Or three? Or two?

I glance out the window and see the way the sun has just faded beyond the buildings surrounding us, and I realize five o'clock is the perfect hour of light in the gardens. We'll take photos there after the ceremony, and then we'll have a special dinner, and then we'll dance and head up to our suite to start the honeymoon.

Suddenly "Canon in D" is playing and I'm walking to the front of the chapel. My dad moves in beside me, and he shakes my hand before he pulls me into a hug. I hear my mom sniffle in the front row.

Ellie and Luke are sitting on my side, and the doors open as Travis escorts Sara down the aisle before she stands in place beside where Tessa will stand when she walks in next. Travis sits beside my mom.

The doors burst open, and there she is.

My bride.

I've never seen a more perfect vision in my life. She's a queen in her white dress as she seemingly floats down the aisle.

Her mom walks beside her, and they're moving achingly slowly. I just want her to get to me. I just want to hold her hands in mine, to say *I do* and slide a ring onto her finger and let the world know that this is the woman I've pledged forever to.

God, I love her. We took the long road to end up in this place, but I couldn't be happier that this is where we are right now in this moment.

Tessa swipes a tear from her cheek, and I find myself doing the same as I take in the vision that she is, as I think about our future together that's just within our grasp, our baby that she's growing now, more babies that will fill the house on the corner and whatever house in Vegas we ultimately choose.

Our future is before us, and all we have to do is exchange the promises.

I shift on my feet as I wait for her to get to me.

Just as the slow-closing hinge on the door does its thing and the door seals us into the room, it swings open again.

My eyes widen as they move beyond Tessa to the three women standing there.

Savannah.

Brandi.

Tiffany.

Brandi? I knew Savannah and Tiffany met each other at the craft fair, and I had a feeling they'd kept in touch.

But how does Brandi figure into any of this?

Tessa stops in the middle of the aisle as she sees my eyes slide away from her and behind her, and she turns seemingly in slow motion to see who's there.

Savannah holds a manila folder in her hands, and all three women are out of breath, as if they ran to get here in time.

"I'm sorry, this is a private event," Gloria tells them quietly, as if all eyes in the room aren't already on them as they interrupt our ceremony.

"Oh, I'm well aware of that, thanks," Savannah says to her with a glare. "But we have some information the groom needs to be made aware of before he marries this…this…this *liar*." She gestures toward Tessa.

"Get out," I hiss through a clenched jaw. "I know exactly who I'm marrying, and you will not ruin this day."

Savannah shakes her head, and my eyes move to Brandi. She won't look at me.

"I have some information you need to be made aware of," Savannah says.

No **MISTAKE**

"That's enough," Janet says, stalking back up the aisle toward Savannah. "Get out of here. All three of you." She shoos them with her hand, but they don't move.

Savannah looks at my would-be mother-in-law with disdain, like she's simply an annoyance standing in her way, and then she huffs as she walks around her and down the aisle toward me.

She laughs as she moves. "Been down an aisle like this before, am I right?" she asks, her eyes laser-focused on me.

"You were the biggest mistake I ever made," I tell her, anger coursing through my veins as she approaches me. I glance at Tiffany, who looks like she's loving every second of this shit fest. "And you aren't far behind."

Savannah stops in front of me. "Well, sweetie, I'm just here to stop you from making another one."

She holds out the envelope to hand it to me, and I bat it away.

"I don't care what's in there. I don't care what you have to say to me. Get the hell out of here. Get the hell out of my *life*."

Savannah tilts her head. "You don't care that you have a child somewhere out there? A little boy who shares your flesh and blood?"

I blow out an exasperated breath as the anger swimming in my veins rises to the surface. God *dammit*. I am so fucking sick of this woman and her manipulations and lies. "Stop making shit up, Savannah! Stop with the lies!"

My eyes fall to Tessa behind her. She's holding the side of her stomach and trying to take in a deep breath, but she's also crying now, which appears to be making the deep breaths a little harder. Her mom takes the bouquet of flowers from her hands and sets them on a chair as she laces an arm around Tessa's waist to hold her up.

"It's not a lie," Savannah says, her voice hard. She opens the envelope and takes some papers out. "This is a copy of a birth certificate dated over seven years ago. Check out the mother's name." She hands me a sheet of paper, and sure enough, Tessa Taylor is listed as the mother.

The date falls in October the year she left me.

Seven months after she left.

There is no father listed.

The name is simply "Baby Boy Taylor."

She hands me another certificate, and I read the words on the top. *Adoption Certificate.*

A chill runs up my spine.

She disappeared seven years ago, and nobody ever really explained why.

Was she pregnant with my child?

Is this true?

Do I have a kid out there that I didn't have any idea about?

I hold the papers in my hands. I step past Savannah, and I walk up to Tessa, whose tears have turned to sobs now.

If it's true…she should be the one to tell me.

Not fucking *Savannah*.

I still don't know why Tiffany and Brandi are here. I still haven't wrapped my brain around how Brandi figures into any of this at all.

What the fuck is happening?

We were so close. So fucking close.

It was all within our grasp.

"Is this true?" I ask, my voice coming out too quietly as I grasp to hang onto some semblance of control. The room seems to spin around me as I try my hardest to focus on Tessa. "Is this why you left our senior year?"

No **MISTAKE**

Janet holds her daughter up as if Tessa's knees are collapsing under her.

Her sob fills the room, and on the tail end of it, I hear the confirmation.

"Yes."

To be concluded in book 5, FAVORITE MISTAKE.

ACKNOWLEDGMENTS

I'll save my acknowledgments for the final book since I know you're ready to get to *Favorite Mistake*… and I can't wait for you to see what's next.

xoxo,
Lisa Suzanne

ABOUT THE AUTHOR

Lisa Suzanne is a romance author who resides in Arizona with her husband and two kids. She's a former high school English teacher and college composition instructor. When she's not cuddling or chasing her kids, she can be found working on her latest book or watching reruns of *Friends*.

ALSO BY LISA SUZANNE

HOME GAME
Vegas Aces Book One
#1 Bestselling Sports Romance

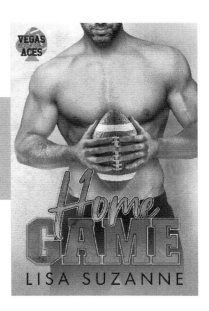

A LITTLE LIKE DESTINY
A Little Like Destiny Book One
#1 Bestselling Rock Star Romance

Printed in Great Britain
by Amazon